NOAH'S BARK
Christine Bush

Dedicated veterinarian Hope Highfield is always rescuing creatures in need, whether they be abandoned or sick animals, lost teenagers, or lonely senior citizens who wear hightop sneakers. She will go to any length for a cause.

But self-made and assertive Noah Brandywine has no intention of being rescued. In fact, he would like to throttle the adorable little woman who has practically brought his multi-million dollar corporation to a screeching halt by implying that Brandywine Beauty Products may be engaging in unethical animal testing.

Nothing in his life has ever mattered more than building his corporate empire—until he has to match wits with Hope Highfield. Is he falling in love with this pint-sized instigator? What will she think when he has to admit that he is petrified of animals—from baby kittens and a mammoth dog, to an errant goat who seems to have a hankering for him? To protect animals from pain and suffering, Hope is willing to risk danger and destruction. What is Noah willing to risk to earn her love and faith?

NOAH'S BARK

•

Christine Bush

AVALON BOOKS
NEW YORK

PRINTED IN THE UNITED STATES OF AMERICA
ON ACID-FREE PAPER
BY HADDON CRAFTSMEN, BLOOMSBURG, PENNSYLVANIA

This book is dedicated to Michelle, Debbie, and Pat, my partners in crime. May you have love and laughter and peace every day of your lives.

Prologue

Ryerstown Daily News,
Thursday Morning Edition

To the editor:

Truth in advertising? Mr. Noah Brandywine, of Brandywine Beauty Products, advertises that his products are developed cruelty-free. But animals sick from testing have been washing up on the shore of the Madison River at my veterinarian clinic, across the river from his plant. "Mr. Makeup Magnate" is much too busy to accept my phone calls to answer my questions.

Our community deserves to know the truth. Are you a liar, Mr. Brandywine? I challenge you to allow me to inspect your plant so that you can prove me wrong. And

1

in the meantime, I'm boycotting all Brandywine Beauty Products until we are sure defenseless animals are not suffering to produce them. It's your move, Noah Brandywine.

Dr. Hope Highfield, D.V.M.

Associated Press Office, Thursday 8:00 P.M.

"Hey, check this out!" The young reporter looked up from his job screening local papers for human interest stories with national appeal. "I think I just saw this guy on Oprah last week! Now this lady veterinarian is calling for a boycott of his products. He's the big wheel from Brandywine Beauty Products. Accused of testing on animals. The tree huggers will love it."

It had been a slow night in the AP office. No new world strife, no impending natural disasters. Now his fingers flew over the keyboard. He filed the information for national distribution onto the AP wire system. The world was waiting for news.

"Okay, Dr. Hope Highfield," he chuckled to himself. "Go get 'em!"

Chapter One

Ryerstown, Pennsylvania, Friday 8:00 A.M.

Just how many ways can you strangle a woman? Noah Brandywine gripped the soft leather of the steering wheel and stomped on the gas pedal of his Jaguar. Just like the ad had promised, it sped silently and smoothly down the road toward "Hope's Haven," home and clinic of the most infuriating veterinarian in the world.

He usually babied the car, treating it like royalty. But today had not been a usual day. From his glass-walled office on the top floor of Brandywine Beauty Products, he had watched in horror as the crowd had gathered outside the door of his plant. Angry citizens, picket signs, those ridiculous news vans—where had they all come from?

"Bring down Brandywine! Bring down Brandywine!" they were chanting. Inside his silk Armani suit, he had begun to sweat.

The phones had been ringing off the wall. "Is it true you are torturing animals in your plant?" "Nationwide, retailers are refusing delivery of your products. Do you have any comment?"

Was this some kind of nightmare?

He had hired Roberta, his gorgeous secretary, for her ability to discourage even the most determined with her icy stare. She had turned that stare on him with the arrival of the first TV news crew.

"I'm giving immediate notice, Mr. Brandywine," the tall blond had said as she gathered her things. Her perfectly made-up face gazed coldly into his. "I don't like bad press. And this is not *my* fault."

She handed him a news clipping of the letter to the editor, and then the picture and article from the front page of *USA Today*. "I simply screened your calls, as I was instructed to do. We do not accept calls from every psychopath who dials the telephone."

She spun on her heel and left the office, leaving behind the expensive scent of Brandywine's "Emotion" perfume. He had a sudden vision of good-smelling rats deserting the ship.

He read. He fumed. Testing on animals? Was everyone out of their minds?

Then he'd snuck out of the office by the freight elevator, avoiding the growing crowd and the hungry news cameras. He wore his golf hat low on his brow. He wore his mirrored sunglasses.

Noah Brandywine, slinking off in a disguise.

He sped off in his Jaguar, mind in a rage. Crossing the river bridge, he slowed the car to a respectable speed. He wished he could slow his pulse as well. Calm and cool and always in control—that was how people described Noah Brandywine, meteoric business success.

But he had handled million-dollar contracts with more savvy than he had handled the situation this morning. With a lifetime of self-discipline behind him, he would fight and win the battle of his emotions. He would take the upper hand. He would confront the sadly misinformed veterinarian who was threatening his empire. And if she didn't agree, a lawsuit instigated by his bevy of attorneys should be effective.

His calm had returned by the time he pulled into the long and rutted driveway that led to "Hope's Haven." The low-slung Jaguar bounced ungraciously on the rough stones. He was eager to end this pothole expedition. He stopped the car within sight of a low, sprawling vet clinic, nestled in wild-flowers and green summer grass. A beat-up Suburban was parked in the drive. He pulled up behind it, and unfolded his six foot-two inch frame from the Jag, straightening his shoulders, feeling powerful.

After all, he was Noah Brandywine, and he was in the right. He would show Hope Highfield who was the boss.

Or so he thought. Until he saw the animals. Real, live animals. Everywhere.

Hope had heard the purr of the car engine when it first turned into the drive. She smiled a self-satisfied smile and waded back to the riverbank, wrapping the tiny kitten she had rescued in the bottom of her oversized sweatshirt to warm it. Across the river, the Brandywine Beauty Products manufacturing plant shined chrome-and-glass bright.

Writing the letter to the paper had been a stroke of genius, after her many phone calls had been so "corporately declined." Now *her* phone was ringing off the hook with calls from reporters from all over the country. She didn't know who she ought to thank for the article in *USA Today,* but when she found out, they were definitely going to be on her Christmas card list! She finally had the famous Mr. Brandywine's undivided attention.

She heard the car scrunch to a stop just as she reached the top of the embankment. She looked up and saw the impeccable grey suit unfold graciously from the low-slung car. And the man. Tall, dark, and handsome. Of course.

She sighed, momentarily remembering that her jeans had

mud on the knees, her wavy dark hair absentmindedly pinned up on the back of her head—well, maybe half up. One piece occasionally drifted past her chin when the breeze blew just right. At five foot-three and a hundred and ten pounds soaking wet (which she often was lately, it seemed), her 2X sweatshirt from the University of Vermont was not exactly a fashion statement.

"Oh well," she said to herself as she clumped toward the visitor, her too-big boots making funny sliding noises as she crossed the gravel.

He was standing very still, which would have registered sooner, if she had not had a momentary short circuit worrying about her bedraggled appearance. In fact, when she really looked at him, the man seemed frozen in place, more or less like a photograph of a model for *Investment Banker's Monthly*. He sure looked good. She walked toward him curiously.

Noah was frozen in place. And he had no intention of moving even a solitary muscle. All around him, like something from his worst nightmare, wild animals paced. And sniffed. Ready to attack. Man, he detested animals!

The first barrage came from kittens. With piercing little meows, like stereophonic sound, two multicolored beasts rubbed themselves against his ankles, suddenly jumping in unison to climb his Armani-clad legs. Their little claws grabbed at him, making him feel like an unwilling victim of acupuncture. With horror, he watched the little snags of silk appear on his formerly pristine suit.

"AGHHH!" he finally yelled, his body moving to action as he stamped his imported Italian leather loafers on the grassy ground, dislodging the culprits before they could climb any higher to do any excruciating damage to any other valuable body parts.

He had won the battle but not the war. The kittens were gone, at least for the moment. But as he looked up in his millisecond of relief, he saw the next enemy coming full speed ahead, in the form of the largest dog that he had ever seen in his life.

Like a slow motion drama, he watched the lumbering black

and white beast approach from the nearby riverbank, feet the size of a medium dinosaur, lolling tongue spewing slobber.

The animal episodes of his life flashed before his eyes . . . the eight-year-old Noah being attacked by the junkyard dog from the dump next to their trailer park . . . the stitches, the rabies shots in the stomach . . . the rats that ran rampant, making noises in the night. . . .

His heart was hammering like a tympani drum as the giant canine bore down upon him.

"No, Gretchen," he heard a melodic voice call out.

Gretchen didn't seem to care. One hundred twenty pounds of carnivorous-looking canine suddenly took flight, aiming right at his middle, like a kamikaze pilot with a mission.

"UGHHH!" he bellowed, as the air was forced from his lungs with the collision. He was flat on his back, pinned to the ground by the enormous paws, Gretchen's massive head looming over him. This was it. He was a goner.

The next thing his mind registered was . . . doggy breath. Gretchen's big lolling tongue slobbered up his cheek, her eyes looked adoringly into his. *Call 911,* he thought. *I'm going to have a heart attack!*

The sound of laughter reached his ears.

"Come on, Gretchen, give the guy a chance." Dinosaur dog agreeably retreated, and went bounding away after a butterfly, tail wagging gaily in the summer sunlight.

He was alive. It was a miracle. He rolled over and pulled himself to his knees, then turned to face the laughter.

"You must be Noah Brandywine," the laughing muddy person said to him. "I'm Dr. Hope Highfield, and I've been expecting you."

"Obviously. You called out the troops."

She laughed again. "Sorry about that inauspicious welcome. At first, I felt uncomfortable to greet you in these muddy work clothes."

His eyes swept over her: giant mud-spotted sweatshirt, enormous boots.

"But I guess you could call Gretchen the great equalizer. You look as bad as me!" She laughed again.

He looked down, horror on his face. His custom made shirt looked like it had been tattooed with giant doggy prints. There were grass stains on his knees. His imported shoes were scuffed.

Fury mounted in him. "You're laughing? This place is a health hazard! First you try to ruin my entire business, then you proceed to ruin my clothes? Let alone scaring me to death! You ought to be committed."

He turned to leave.

"Wait," she called out, not laughing now, but her eyes still twinkling. She didn't want him to go. "Don't worry, I'll pay to have your suit cleaned. Gretchen didn't mean any harm. She was just being overly friendly."

"Overly friendly? You ought to donate her to the government to be used as our next secret weapon. And those vicious cats that attacked me . . ."

"The eight-week-old kittens? Couldn't hurt a fly. Want one? Someone just dropped them off this morning and I'm trying to find homes."

"Not me. I could live my entire life without ever coming in contact with an animal, and that would suit me just fine."

Her face became serious.

"Dislike them enough to sacrifice them to unethical testing, Mr. Brandywine? Are you responsible for this damage?"

She stepped toward him, then, her hands uncovering the dampened ball of fur that she had wrapped in the bottom of her sweatshirt. It was a tiny grey kitten, smaller than the ones he had already tangled with. It was barely moving, and its eyes looked dull and pained. He saw the shaved back, with rows of colored dots visible.

Animal detester or not, his heart lurched at the sight of the sick kitten.

"That's horrible. Is that what you're talking about? Someone is running tests on animals like this?"

"We fish them out of the river. Some are already dead. Some survive. It's got to stop. You've got to stop."

"Me?" he barked in outrage. He tried to ignore the tears that were welling up in the vet's eyes. "Me?" he repeated. He wanted to stay angry, but there was something about the tiny woman in front of him that had touched him. "You find this . . . tragedy . . . and you automatically decide that Brandywine Beauty Products is responsible?"

"Your plant is right across the river. You office wouldn't take my phone calls—"

"There are several plants across the river. These animals could have come from any of them. And I didn't even know you had called. I'm out of town a lot for publicity campaigns these days, we're launching a new line . . ."

"So maybe someone in your plant is launching these animals while you are off launching your new line."

"Never. Absolutely not. I run a tight ship. Nothing like that could ever go on at Brandywine."

"Will you let me inspect the plant?"

"Out of the question. I will not be bulldozed into looking like an unfeeling culprit."

"If the shoe fits . . ."

Out of the corner of his eye, he noticed more animals lingering. There were several full grown cats, one almost the size of a small lion. And slowly approaching, white spiky tufts of hair protruding everywhere, was a goat. His palms felt sweaty. He didn't know how much more of this he could take.

"I'm just not as enthralled with animals as you are. But that doesn't mean I want them hurt, Dr. Highfield."

Looking down, he spotted his wallet laying in the grass, where it had evidently fallen during his acrobatic feat with Gretchen. He bent over to pick it up.

"Uh, oh," he heard the musical voice of Dr. Wild Kingdom belatedly exclaim. "Don't bend over like that. Watch out for Billie—"

If he had ever wondered what it was like to be hit by a train, his curiosity would have been fulfilled. Billie the wandering goat had scoped out his position and attacked in a flash. Head down, hooves pounding with speed, his butting head made direct contact with Noah's protruding posterior.

THUD!

He went flying though the air and landed face down in the

grass. Unbelievable. And the incorrigible Dr. Highfield was laughing again. He looked around. The errant goat was nowhere in sight. He didn't want another close encounter with the beast.

"I tried to warn you," Hope gasped. "We all know never to bend over when Billie is around."

"Billie the Goat. Original. I'm glad you find it so amusing." He brushed off his suit, trying to rescue his fleeting dignity.

"I'll be going now, Dr. Highfield. But I want you to know that I will not stand for any more character assassinations from you. I have never—and would never—use animals for testing of any kind. I want nothing to do with animals. And after this day, I am more sure of that than ever."

He took a few long strides back to his car, his bones feeling like they weren't strung together exactly right. He was going to be stiff, for sure.

He had left the windows of the Jag open when he had arrived, he saw to his dismay when he approached the car. He had found the Billie the Goat.

"No!" he yelled, waving his arms frantically. The goat had his head inside the open car window, and was calmly chewing on the expensive leather upholstery of his top-of-the-line, special order bucket seat.

"Billie, no!" hollered Hope, running toward the goat. She wasn't laughing anymore. "I'm so sorry. I'm so sorry." The goat hobbled a few feet away and stood looking at him. He could have sworn the goat was grinning. "I will pay to fix the upholstery—and for the suit. . . ." Her face was flushed; two red dots stood out on her cheeks.

"You certainly will," he replied in his "million dollar deal" voice. "And you will pay for a lot more when my attorneys get through with you." He gracefully climbed into the Jag, and started the engine. He forced his voice to stay even. "Goodbye, Dr. Highfield."

He left a trail of dust.

He was furious. He was sore. She was the biggest pain in the butt he had ever met, and in twenty-four short hours, she had practically ruined his life. But she had also made his pulse race, a little voice acknowledged, from somewhere deep in his mind.

And why, when he watched her forlorn face, standing by the side of the driveway holding the soggy kitten, did he feel like such a cad?

What a mess! As the car pulled out of sight Hope turned around and headed for the clinic. She had met with the austere Noah Brandywine, and she hadn't accomplished a thing—except maybe to make him more resolute than ever to ignore her pleas. Why did Billie have to decide to lunch on his car upholstery? That was going to cost her a mint!

She dried the kitten and gave her some milk. Safe from the river, and in loving hands, the little creature began to purr. She put her in a large box by her desk that held other kittens the same age. Instantly, the kitten snuggled up with the others. Well, another one was saved.

Noah Brandywine. She thought of the smiling, impeccably dressed man who was at the very apex of Brandywine Beauty Products. She had even seen him on Oprah.

She suppressed a wicked grin. He had looked a little different from his public image by the time Gretchen and Billie had been through with him. Like he had been put through a blender.

He had really been afraid. How could such a powerful and successful man be so afraid of animals? The thought made her sad.

Hope loved animals. Growing up in the Highfield mansion in the high society section of Philadelphia, having a pet had been absolutely out of the question. Her parents' elegant house had been more like a museum than a family home. And the formal Highfield lifestyle precluded anything so "frivolous" as a cat or a dog.

She remembered her father's rage when she announced her intention to become a veterinarian. He had other plans for his heiress daughter, and he had controlled her actions with his authoritarian ways for most of her life.

But she didn't falter in her choice to make her own decision about her career, even when it meant giving up her inheritance. She had never regretted it.

And now she had more pets than she knew what to do with. She rescued them, healed them, enjoyed them, and sometimes helped place them in loving homes. What would it be like to be afraid of animals? She just couldn't imagine it. And she also couldn't get the tall, dark, handsome, mudspeckled makeup magnate out of her mind.

She caught a glimpse of herself in the bathroom mirror as she walked by, and gasped. She really did look awful. It was one thing to be obsessed about looks, it was another to go to the other extreme—which sometimes she admitted she did. When was the last time she had worn clothes that fit? When was the last time she had taken the time to style her hair? And most importantly, why was she suddenly thinking about these things? She refused to think that it had anything to do with Mr. Pompous-Afraid-of-a-Cat. She was not out to impress anybody.

But she *could* take a shower and wash off the river mud. In her apartment in the back of the clinic, she peeled off the grungy clothing and tossed it into the hamper. The sweatshirt was one of her favorites. A client had given it to her as payment for spaying his cat. Which wasn't that unusual.

The pets that she treated were often owned by eccentric country folk who rarely used cash in their transactions. No matter how poor, these proud country people would find some ingenious way to reimburse her for her services. She had received farm fresh eggs, home canned peaches, a butter churn, assorted sweatshirts, a TV antenna, a kitchen sink, and several coupons for free tattoos.

The shower was hot and relaxing. She shampooed her hair with gusto, and wrapped herself in a thick terry bathrobe when she was finished. In bare feet, she padded out to the kitchen, feeling clean and refreshed.

"Hope! Help!" The yell came from the driveway outside the clinic. The voice was deep, and full—and panicked, and she knew it instantly. Noah Brandywine was back. She flew out the door.

His day had gone from bad to worse. He had left Hope's Haven behind him, filthy, battered, and smelling a bit like a goat. But he hadn't gotten far. Less than a mile down the winding country road, he had discovered two things. Feeling sharp little needles pricking his ankles, he had looked down to discover a stowaway kitten in his car. A fluffy ball of fur—bearing daggers, which she was rhythmically digging into his legs. He cursed silently.

He had to return the kitten. It would be just like Hope Highfield to alert the media that he had kidnapped one of her pathetic creatures, implying that he would be using it for dastardly experiments in his secret laboratories. Dr. Frankenstein on the loose. He banged his fist against the steering wheel in frustration.

But when he had pulled the car over to extract the feline's attack-paws from his skin, he had discovered horror number two. Bounding down the road after the Jaguar, with spiky fur flying, came Billie the Goat. With the car stopped, the goat caught up, banging his head determinedly into the rear bumper. Double kidnapping. He was in deep trouble.

He climbed out of the car, trying to figure out what to do.

A car drove past, its occupants staring at him curiously.

Never seen a man with a goat before, buddy? he wanted to scream. But he didn't.

Face to face with Billie the Goat, he considered his options. The list wasn't long. He had to return *both* the animals to Hope's Haven. Pronto. He approached the bulldozer on legs hesitatingly, glad to see he wore a collar. He'd put the goat into the car, speed back to the clinic, and get rid of both pets. The goat was observing him with moonlike eyes. He stared back. He'd never really seen a goat before. He'd never really *smelled* a goat before. Disgusting.

He put out a tentative hand and grabbed the collar. Billie came willingly. He opened the passenger door of the Jag. The goat obediently climbed in, standing precariously on the passenger seat. Noah shut the door.

See, I can do this, he congratulated himself, ignoring the flashes of fear that ran through him.

But then the goat nonchalantly crossed over the gear shift, his hooves clacking horribly on the console, hopped onto the driver's seat, and then right out the driver's door on the other side of the car. Billie turned and looked at him.

Catch me if you can, his smirking goat face said.

He did. But it wasn't easy. The goat ran laps around the car at a speed that would be envied at the Indy. Finally, Noah stopped abruptly, and spun around. He caught the errant goat as it came up behind him on his next lap, throwing his arms around the scruffy neck. *Whew! What a smell!*

This time he kept the passenger door shut, putting Billie in through the driver's door, and climbing in right behind him. He was leaving nothing to chance. He shut the windows. No escape. But the smell was threatening to knock him out.

He raced the engine, turned the car around, and headed back for the vet clinic, swearing under his breath. The little kitten had emerged from under the seat. A minor goat versus cat fight ensued. The goat won, proudly sitting up in the passenger seat, surveying the view as they sped by.

The kitten, now slighted doused in goat saliva, had climbed up his arm, perching precariously on his shoulder as he drove. A car passed, its driver staring. The kitten was making a strange rumbling noise in his ear, sounding slightly like a race car engine needing a tuneup. Noah prayed for the nightmare to end. He was in a cold sweat.

For the second time, the Jag bounded down the uneven lane that led to the clinic. This time, he didn't even try to avoid the potholes. The shortest distance between two points is a straight line.

He jerked the car to a stop outside the clinic office door, leaping out of the car and sucking in a much-needed breath of fresh air. "Hope! Help!" he cried out, at the end of his rope, kitten and goat now bounding out of the car. The door banged and she appeared.

"Noah!" she exclaimed, her quick eyes registering the situation. "They followed you?"

He nodded numbly, his eyes locked onto hers. "I brought them back."

She didn't laugh, which made him grateful. She seemed to sense his trauma. "Good job, Noah. Thanks."

He wanted to touch her then, seeing her standing there in a fluffy pink robe, barefooted, with wet, clean hair dancing around her shoulders and her face looking so kind. Was there anything under that barely tied robe?

He brought himself up shortly, disgusted with his testosterone-ridden thoughts. First of all, he looked like a mess, and he smelled like a goat. Secondly, the alluring little package in pink was the person who was practically ruining his business with her accusations, and was responsible for the creatures that had made his life hell. Was he nuts?

Something nudged his leg, and he looked down with renewed horror to find Billie the Goat by his side, looking up at him adoringly.

"What's wrong with this goat?" he croaked. "Why is he looking at me like that?"

Hope was laughing now. "It's a she. Billie is short for Wilhelmina. I think she's in love."

Noah was at his breaking point. He spun around without a word, and climbed back into his smelly, upholstery-chewed Jaguar that now needed a major wheel alignment. He was getting out of this crazy place.

He roared down the lane, still seeing Hope in the rear view mirror, standing in the sunlight, like an alluring, irrepressible mirage in pink. He swallowed hard. What a day! What else could happen? He decided to avoid the media at the plant in his present condition, going straight home to repair the damages and to work out a plan to counteract the accusations against him. Noah Brandywine had to get back in control. No more surprises.

There was a sudden odor in the air, mingled with the lingering aroma of goat. He looked down at the floor mat on the passenger side of the car. Well, one more surprise. The kitten had left him a present. Man, did he hate animals!

Chapter Two

Noah went straight home. He stripped his clothes off in the garage and plunked them, shoes and all, into the shining aluminum trash can. There was no redeeming those clothes, and to tell the truth, he didn't want any memories of the last few esteem-stealing hours lying around. He was going to get his life back into order.

The hot shower felt good. He shaved again, even though he didn't need it. He'd simply start his day once more from the beginning. Take Two! When he emerged a few minutes later, dressed in another expensive suit selected from his well-stocked closet, he was beginning to feel like himself again. A little stiff, but smelling good! The scent of the exclusive Brandywine aftershave bolstered his spirits. So much better than "Eau de Goat."

The house, which sat high over the riverbank, up the river

from the plant, was an architectural masterpiece. Gleaming white walls and lots of glass, it was sleek and immaculate, a place to be proud of, which he was. Pretty good for a poor kid who had once lived in a rusty trailer by the town dump! His mother would be proud. He suddenly stretched, swallowing the lump that threatened to form in his throat. Back to business.

He perched on the white leather sofa, portable phone in his hand. He made arrangements for a replacement car to be delivered, the Jag picked up to be repaired and detailed. Goat smell gone forever.

He called his office. An efficient, personable voice greeted him. His capable office manager had wasted no time in replacing the icy Roberta. "This is Noah Brandywine, your boss." He proceeded to give detailed instructions on what he wanted accomplished before he arrived back at his office.

He ran a tight ship, with loyal employees. He knew how to achieve success, how to win.

"And please alert the media. Print, radio, and television. Have the PR team set up the conference room. I will be in at four this afternoon, for a press conference. We'll put an end to this thing once and for all." His voice exuded charm and confidence.

"Certainly, Mr. Brandywine," she said efficiently. "We'll be ready for you."

He hung up the phone and took a deep breath, exhaling it slowly.

"Watch out, Dr. Hope Highfield. You're going to see what happens when you tangle with Noah Brandywine." He pushed every thought of the pink robe out of his mind.

He dialed one more phone number. It was picked up on the first ring. "Frank," he said to the gruff voice of his security chief, Frank Johnson, when he answered, "Get me information on this Dr. Hope Highfield. Pronto."

"Give me one hour," replied the voice. Then the line went dead.

Noah sat on the white leather couch and waited.

* * *

Flashbulbs were exploding, and the noise level in the conference room rose to a crescendo as Noah Brandywine entered at 4:05 P.M. His staff had done their job. The room was packed.

He took the microphone at the podium, his face smiling and composed, appearance immaculate, the epitome of the Brandywine image. His raised hand hushed the crowd.

"Thank you all for coming at such short notice. I wish to read a statement, ladies and gentlemen," he said personably. Glancing casually at the crowd, he acknowledged an elderly woman perched in the front row, pencil poised over a tablet. "Well, hello, Griselda," he said cheerfully aside, "How are things at *HomeLife* Magazine?"

The blue-haired matron smiled, a four-decade veteran of the publishing business. She knew posturing when she saw it, and let him get away with it. "Just fine, Mr. B. And what do you have for us today? Quite a stink stirred up out there . . ."

"So true. And that is, of course, what I wish to address." Every eye was on him. "First of all, may I state directly and without any hesitation that Brandywine Beauty Products is not, will not, and has never participated in any type of research or testing involving animals, as recently erroneously implied by Dr. Hope Highfield. As you all know, we pride ourselves on our ethical, community-based business procedures, and would never abuse the trust of our customers, both locally and worldwide. This is, of course, a serious accusation, and we have done everything in our power to discover why Dr. Highfield insisted upon undermining our well-respected reputation in this way. Our investigation has uncovered a sadly personal motivation for her attack. Dr. Highfield is the estranged daughter of shipping magnate Marshall Highfield, who has recently been unsuccessful in his company's bid for the Brandywine Beauty shipping contract. Evidently, in her misguided attempt to return to her father's good graces, she hoped to maneuver Brandywine into reconsidering the shipping contract."

There was a mumbling throughout the crowd.

"No, no," he said with an understanding smile. "We are planning to press no charges at this time, as long as this unfortunate and disagreeable incident can be put to rest. We will stand on our own excellent reputation and continue business as usual. Thank you again for your attendance. That's all for today."

His smile flashed, and he turned and exited the room as voices exploded behind him.

He was back in control.

Are you still smiling, Dr. Hope Highfield? he thought as he returned to his quiet office. He imagined the twinkle leaving her eyes in an instant, and then he frowned. Winning didn't seem to feel quite as good as he thought it would.

Hope was down on her knees, methodically scrubbing out pet cages with her eighteen-year-old assistant Manuel, when the evening news came on the television. Noah Brandywine's press conference was the lead story of the day. She jerked her head up at the sound of his name, just in time to see a close-up of his well-groomed face filling the television screen.

". . . erroneously implied by Dr. Hope Highfield . . ." ". . . estranged daughter of shipping magnate Marshall Highfield. . . ." ". . . a misguided attempt to return to his good graces. . . ."

Dr. Hope Highfield began to sputter. "Why of all the—How could he—How dare he—" Her face had turned bright red, and she banged her head on the top of a cage when she suddenly tried to stand up.

"Hey, Hope," called Manny from his position across the floor, "don't have a coronary on that idiot's account. He ain't worth it."

"*Isn't* . . ." she said automatically, lost in her own thoughts. "Isn't worth it."

"Isn't," he parroted with a lopsided grin. "You want I should call in my old homeys to do a little work on his face? We could put a most definite end to his press conference career."

Hope sighed, acting like she was considering his suggestion, and then laughed. "No, Manny, your homeys are retired. We're going to figure this one out on our own. But thanks for sticking up for me!"

She smiled at the young man who had grown so much since he had appeared on her doorstep two years before as a runaway. He had worked part time for her since that day. He had also finished high school, reconciled with his parents, and applied for college, where he was headed in the fall.

"So what about your old man? Where'd that guy get this story?"

"*Not* from my father, you can be sure."

She picked up the telephone and dialed. "Johnston? This is Hope. Is my father in?"

In seconds, her father's commanding voice was on the line.

"Hope Elizabeth, how delightful to hear the sound of your voice."

"Watch the news, Father?"

"Certainly. I got quite a kick out of it. The very thought of you sniveling around to get back into my good graces did my old heart good."

"I don't snivel." She laughed out loud.

"Obviously. That's because you are what is affectionately known as a "brick head," one of the more stubborn cusses that exist on the planet. Determined to fight all foes, to save the world . . ."

"It's wonderful to hear that we're not estranged, father, sniveling or not!"

"We simply agree to disagree, Hope Elizabeth. You've made it plenty clear over the years that you want to make your own decisions. You are simply out of my will, until you come to your senses. Not that you care. After what you did with your grandmother's inheritance . . ."

"The SPCA sincerely appreciated the donation."

"And that ridiculous career minding wild animals. . . ."

"I'm a board certified veterinarian."

"Always saving some pathetic thing or another. How's that demented boy, by the way?"

Hope grinned. "Manuel's wonderful. Starts college in the fall." Across the room, Manny grinned widely.

The old man sighed into the phone. "Well, I guess they don't make colleges like they used to."

"Is it true, Father? About the Brandywine shipping contract?"

He grunted into the phone. "Young whippersnapper. We did lose the contract. But I don't see that you and this animal nonsense have anything to do with it. Nothing I'd like better than to teach him a lesson, though. Would you like some assistance on this?"

Hope laughed. "No thanks, Father. I can fight my own battles."

"Don't I just know it!" he conceded.

"Actually, I'm not even totally sure he's the culprit. I was just firing a test shot. But his response riled me up. He was so busy trying to discredit me, he didn't even address the issue of the animals. But I'll take care of him."

"So, then, are you planning to save this one, too?"

"Save Noah Brandywine? Whatever for?" she asked in a mystified voice.

"You truly are a brick head, Hope Elizabeth," the old man growled, and the phone went dead.

"We have to have a plan." Hope paced the floor, stuffing popcorn into her mouth.

"You're wearing a hole, Doc," Manny griped from his spot on the couch. "Park it."

She sat.

"There's truth to what Noah says, you know." She looked up into the air as she spoke, watching the parrot who was precariously perched on the curtain rod.

"You mean you *are* trying to get back into your father's good graces?"

She threw popcorn at him. The bird swooped from the rod and gobbled it up.

"No, Manny. My father doesn't have any good graces. He just has money. What I'm trying to say is that Noah's comment about not being the only factory on the river is true. There are several more. It's only fair, don't you think, that I check them out before dumping on him anymore?"

"You going soft, Doc?"

Another popcorn storm made for a happy parrot.

"I'm tough as nails. But I'm fair. So I have to check out the other possibilities."

"I think you like the guy. I can tell."

"You're insane. I just need to get *all* the information.

Manny grunted. "Jeez, I can just picture the phone call now. 'Hello, unsuspecting target, this is Hope Highfield calling to get you to admit you are torturing poor defenseless animals. Speak clearly into the microphone, please. . . .'"

She made a face. "You're right. Too high profile. This is an—undercover job."

"Oh, Jeez," Manny said, putting his hands on his face. "Something tells me I'm going to barely live to regret this."

It was a hour later when Hope had her first brainstorm. "I've got it," she exclaimed, looking up from the copy of the Ryerstown Daily News she was reading. "I'm starting with "Dirt-busters," which is right up the river. They're advertising for a receptionist! I'll apply for the job, and that will get me into the plant to snoop around and look for signs of unethical research."

"This plan will get you into a padded cell at the state hospital, if you ask me." Manny looked at her with disgust. "A receptionist? Who'd even consider you?"

"I can type. I can answer phones. I'll use a different name. Elizabeth Field."

"News flash. You don't look like a receptionist, Hope. No insult intended. Receptionists look good. Like they wear lots of makeup and wear heels and have those long dagger red nails, and lots of big hair. You know, they look hot!" He looked exasperated.

"If you're trying to get a raise, you need to go to charm school." She frowned at him.

He looked back, silently.

"Well, maybe I would need to jazz myself up just a little

bit," she conceded. "After all, it would be like a disguise, right? I could do that."

"It's a stupid idea. But I've seen worse. One time this dude in my gang had to dress up like a woman to . . ."

"I don't think I want to hear this," she interrupted.

"Right. Okay. I'll get the makeup and shoes from my girl-friend tomorrow. You can apply for the job, but I'm waiting outside in the parking lot when you go in, no matter what you say."

"It'll be like an adventure. Like James Bond . . . or Columbo." She laughed.

"More like Bozo the Clown, if you ask me," he said under his breath.

"I heard that."

"Just answer one question, Doc. Why don't you leave this alone? You've stirred up enough trouble now, and sooner or later the truth will come out. Is it that important to you now to prove that this Brandywine joker is innocent? He seems like a jerk to me."

She thought suddenly of the look in his eyes when he had climbed out of the car with the goat. Something had stirred inside of her. No, he was not a jerk. Mad as she was about his press conference, she couldn't get those eyes out of her mind. For some strange reason, it *was* very important to her that Noah Brandywine was not guilty.

"I'm just trying to be fair," she said lightly to her assistant. "This is a good plan. It would be crazy not to look into all the possibilities, right?"

"Let's not start throwing the term 'crazy' around lightly, Okay, Doc? Most especially not in the same breath as this plan."

Hope Highfield laughed, the sound ringing in the night air. "A girl's got to do what a girl's got to do."

Manuel smiled and just shook his head.

Things like this just didn't happen to James Bond.

Her expedition had started smoothly enough. When she arrived at Dirtbusters at four in the afternoon, inquiring about employment, she had been politely directed to the Personnel Department. Walking in the four-inch heels without breaking her neck had been the biggest challenge. A straight-faced woman with little half-glasses perched on her nose had left her alone to fill out an application for the receptionist position.

She picked up her pen to write as the woman left the room, and immediately popped off two of the artificial nails that she and Manny had glued to her fingertips. How did people write with nails like that? She left the pen, application, and errant nail tips on the desk and slipped out the door. No time to waste. She followed the corridor signs that said "To the Plant."

The wobbly heels slowed her down, so she slid the shoes off and carried them. She had timed her visit for the end of the production day. When she pushed open the door of the plant, she was greeted by the sound of the last machines grinding to a halt as they were turned off. Most of the employees had gone for the day; the few lingering made comments to each other as they gathered up their belongings. No one noticed her as she stood behind packing boxes, getting her bearings.

The air smelled of cleaning products, antiseptic and pine scented. Dirtbusters made floor cleaners, laundry detergents, and bath soap, and if they were testing their products on animals, she was going to find out. Some of the overhead lighting was switched off with a noisy click. The night lights remained on, casting dim shadows amid the large machines and stacks of boxes. Quietly, she crept through the plant, avoiding voices and searching for . . . she had no idea what.

Moving along the perimeter of the large open factory space, she began opening the doors located occasionally along the wall. She found several storage rooms, bathrooms, and employee lockers. There was absolutely nothing suspicious. And then she saw the cat.

Her adrenaline soared. He was a full-sized tiger cat, sleek and strong looking, moving stealthily toward her from across the production floor. Larger by far than the small animals she had rescued from the river, there was still something vaguely familiar about the cat. The coloring? Had they bred cats for their experiments? The thought sickened her.

She bent and pet him, and he purred and rubbed against her leg. Then abruptly, he turned and walked away. Hope (alias Bond) was in fast, barefoot pursuit. He moved around the machinery. Hope moved around the machinery. He climbed up over the machinery. Hope climbed up over the machinery. Somewhere in the pursuit, she dropped her shoes. The cat jumped in and out of large empty cartons, almost daring Hope to follow.

Her knees were bruised. Her pantyhose were a shambles. And the cat was playing with her. She was ready to give up, when the cat suddenly darted for a door on the far side of the plant. In the bottom of the door was a swinging "cat door." The cat disappeared.

Hope groaned her disappointment. On her knees, she stuck her head in through the small opening to see what was there. Blackness greeted her. And the smell of cat. Had she found something?

She couldn't fit through the small opening. Standing again, she reached for the door handle. As it turned in her hand, there was a sudden noise behind her, making her jump. A door banged. The sound of someone whistling could be heard, approaching quickly.

She opened the door with a yank, and jumped inside, barely avoiding being discovered. The door shut solidly behind her. Belatedly, she discovered there was no handle on the inside. She was trapped.

Heart pounding, she moved around carefully in the darkness, investigating. This was no secret laboratory. She was in a small cleaning closet, stashed along with assorted mops and brooms and buckets. There were feeding dishes on the floor for the cat. A litter box sat in one corner. She felt like a fool. No one was experimenting on animals at Dirtbusters.

She heard the whistler walk past the door, and move away. She felt the cat slither up next to her in the darkness, and she bent and scratched his friendly head. Her hair had fallen down around her shoulders.

"You stinker," she said softly, "You got us trapped in here!"

The cat made a small sound that sounded disconcertingly like "Oh yeah?" and took a leap through the cat door.

"OK," she said to herself, "You got *me* trapped in here."

So she sat in the closet, huddled in the dark, and considered her options. She was shoeless, filthy, trespassing and carrying no ID. She could stay until morning, trying to sneak out when the closet door was eventually opened. She could plead insanity . . . amnesia. . . . Candid Camera. But she knew that an impatient Manny sat in the parking lot, and would soon be making a fuss. She was going to have to start yelling and throw herself on the mercy of the "whistler," and get it over with.

But suddenly the cat was back. He slipped through the cat door, then back out again. He sat immediately outside the closet door, and started yeowling with the most screeching tone she had ever heard in a cat.

"Yeooowwwllll!" "Yeoowwllll!" He sounded like he was being tortured. Bad enough being discovered—were people going to think she was torturing the cat?

Frantically she crawled across the closet floor toward the door. "Shhhh! Shhhh!" she called to the cat. The yeowling continued, even escalated.

Desperate, she stuck her head out of the cat door, coming face to face with the cat. "Shhhh!" she said firmly. "YEOWLLLLL!" the cat said more firmly.

And then there was the laughing scratchy voice of an old man. "Well, hello, Dr. Highfield! I didn't know you made house calls!"

The door was opened, and she was freed, standing to face a laughing Manny, and Norman Bright, the night watchman, whom she recognized as one of her clients.

"So waddaya think of Cleo, the Watch-Cat?" the old man chuckled. "Best mouser this company ever had, doncha think?"

"Remember Cleo, Doc," asked Manny, attempting to discipline his face into a serious expression before she kicked him in the shins, "Norman brought him in last year for neutering, says he's been doing great ever since!"

She knew that cat had looked familiar. And she'd wonder forever if that jaunt through the company machinery he'd led her on had been motivated by playfulness or a feline form of revenge!

"I explained about checking for the research animals, Doc." Manny went on. "This place is clear. And I think we can count on Norman keeping an eye on things here for us."

Norman puffed importantly, nodding with commitment.

If Manuel Perez doesn't become a politician some day, she thought dryly, he'll be wasting his talents.

The ride home was quick, and mercifully silent. Her murderous look at Manny's laughing eyes when he got a glimpse of her bare feet and tangled hair was enough to keep his comments short.

"There will be interesting gossip at Dirtbusters," he said chuckling, "When they discover the pair of red high-heel shoes in the plant, and a trail of lost fingernails." She looked down at her hands, noticing for the first time that she had lost every one of the artificial nails in her escapade.

When they pulled into the long drive to Hope's Haven, Hope was dreaming of a hot bath and a quiet ending to the horrible day. But that was not to be. A sleek, newly repaired Jaguar was sitting in the drive waiting for her.

Chapter Three

Noah Brandywine was leaning against the car, one foot casually crossed over the other, arms folded across his chest. Hope sighed as she looked at him. The moonlight was reflecting off the shiny bumper of the car.

"Oh my," she sighed, under her breath. "He looks good enough to eat."

"Did you want the fries or a baked potato with that?" Manny laughed, his sharp ears picking up her comment.

She blushed to the roots of her tangled hair. "Stow it, Manuel. It was a moment of weakness."

She opened the car door and tumbled out, barefoot, rumpled mini-skirt, hair looking like a bird had tried to use it for a nest. Nothing like looking your best when you had to deal with a "picture perfect man." Whatever he wanted, she would face him and get it over with. She tiptoed over the rocky drive in her bare feet.

"Mr. Brandywine," she said in her most cordial, professional tone, her voice belying the fact that she looked like a refugee and was walking like a small child caught on a hot beach. "What brings you to Hope's Haven at this hour? Don't you have a press conference or some important thing to attend to? Cooking up some more inaccurate slander, or a libel and lettuce sandwich maybe?"

As she came near, Noah could see her clearly in the moonlight.

"What happened to you?" he gasped. "Were you in an accident?"

Behind her, she could hear Manny snickering, and she wanted to wring his neck.

"Night, Manny. You can head home now." She spoke through slightly clenched teeth. "I'll see you in the morning."

"Are you sure, Doc?" He was barely containing a laugh. "I don't mind staying—and I can check the animals, especially Georgia . . ."

"Good night."

"Good night, double-o-seven!" He laughed and saluted, as he climbed onto his bike and started peddling down the long drive.

"Double-o-seven? As in James Bond?"

She turned back to Noah.

"The one and only."

"Want to talk about it?"

"I'd rather bungee jump with a cord that's too long, thank you." She grimaced. "Now, honestly, what brings you here? It's been a long day, and I've still got a lot to do."

He was staring at her, and his face looked very serious.

"Actually, Dr. Highfield, we have unfinished business."

Her eyes opened wide. The guy had nerve.

"After that press conference? I'd say we have nothing to talk about, unless you want to confess to your schemes about testing on animals."

"No confession, Doctor." One side of his mouth turned up into a meek smile. Hope found it hopelessly appealing, and she wanted to kick herself for her reaction. "But maybe an apology. For my press conference. For hitting you at a personal level—that stuff about your father. I'm assuming you saw it."

"I saw it."

He was apologizing? She was speechless. Brandywine and apology seemed like an oxymoron.

He went on. "I was misinformed. I mean, the facts were right about the shipping contract, but that father stuff . . . well, I was wrong. I got a phone call from your father—"

Hope started to sputter. "My father? He called you? Why did he do a thing like that?" She was furious, and Noah was smiling.

"He said you'd have that reaction when you learned he'd called. Said something about being an independent brick head."

Hope let air out through clenched teeth.

"Then he wished me luck. What did he mean by that?"

She was fuming. How like her father to wish luck to her enemy. He probably lived for the day he could say "I told you so" to prove the choices she made for her life were wrong. She pushed the angry thoughts away.

Then, determined, she stepped around Noah Brandywine, ignoring him, and plunked her feet into the oversized boots that sat on the doorstep. Without a word, she started clumping toward the kennel building, leaving him standing in the driveway.

"Hey, Hope," he called, turning and following her. "No need to get in a huff. Seriously, I didn't come here to fight with you, I came here to talk . . ."

"You talked. Now go." She didn't turn around. She pulled the door of the kennel building open and stepped inside, letting it bang behind her.

Noah hesitated for a fraction of a second, then followed her into the building. She had turned the lights on. He was in a small room, and Hope was not in sight. Two cats sat on the windowsill. The smell of animals assaulted him. Many animals. He swallowed.

Hope heard the door open and shut and came back to the entryway.

"Look, Mr. Brandywine. We really have nothing worthwhile to talk about. I have animals to tend to for the night, and a very pregnant Great Dane named Georgia who is showing signs that she is ready to drop a difficult litter of puppies. I do not have the time or inclination to speak about my father with you. If you two have such a close relationship, I would suggest perhaps you do lunch—"

He started to laugh.

She wanted to cry.

It was ridiculous. She was insulting him, standing there in a bright red miniskirt, bare legs protruding from the oversized boots, her hair half up, half down, and looking like a bird's nest, her eye makeup smeared. She looked like a small child caught dabbling in her mother's clothes and makeup.

And yet, the sudden unhappy look in her eyes brought him up short, piercing his heart and making him want to reach out to her. Who was this complex person who could have such an effect on him—anger, laughter . . . tenderness? He was used to logic, security, and control. These sudden flashes of emotion were unfamiliar and uncomfortable.

Just leave his mind instructed.

"Could I help you?" his voice said. Was there a short circuit in his brain?

She gave a tired smile. She was actually grateful and touched by his offer, despite her anger at his reference to her father. After all, he'd said her father had called *him,* and not the other way around. And she knew her father's machinations, better than anyone. But she remembered the tortured look in Noah's face when confronted by her bevy of animals earlier in the day. He was afraid of animals. Not a candidate for assistance in a veterinary clinic, that was for sure!

"Thanks," she said softly. "But I can tell you're not comfortable with animals. I appreciate the offer though, especially since we seem to be continually at each other's throats."

His mind flashed the sudden vision, then, of being at Hope Highfield's throat, and he sucked in his breath and licked his lips. He could almost taste the softness of her skin. He was shocked at himself.

She was looking at him quizzically, so he steeled himself. What was happening to him? *Go. Leave. Say goodnight,* said his mind.

"But I'd like to see your clinic," said his voice.

Her eyes lit up. "Okay," she said, watching him closely. "I'll show you around."

Now you've done it, you dope, his mind chastised him. *Let's see how brave you are when you have to face the animals.*

Somehow, he would muster the courage to face the animals, just as long as he could stay close to that neck! Noah swallowed hard, and followed Hope through the door.

The first room in the kennel building housed small pets, some recuperating from surgery or illness. She checked each roomy cage, and her gentle voice and hands comforted the small inhabitants. He carried a large water tank, and watched while she delivered fresh water by hose to each animal's dish.

"Most of these guys will go home tomorrow or the next day," she said quietly. "Except for those in the last section here." She pointed to the cage holding small kittens, healthy now, but still bearing the shaved spots where they had been used for testing. "I'm trying to find homes for them."

He nodded but didn't speak.

She watched him carefully.

"You okay? You look pale."

"I'm fine. Keep going." And he was, watching these small creatures, all confined in cages. They were actually . . . cute.

They had reached the door to the next section of the kennel.

"These are the bigger ones," she said.

The barking began as soon as the door opened. He broke out in a sweat.

There were dogs of assorted sizes in kennels on either side of the small hallway. They jumped, they leaped, they spun in circles. They were excited to see Hope. She entered each cage and delivered food, clean bedding, and substantial hugs and

pats. Noah stood frozen to the spot, watching her in amazement.

She watched his bewildered stare, and her heart filled with
compassion. She found such joy in the simple acceptance and
companionship of animals. What would life be like if she had
never experienced that joy? What if she felt only fear?

"These are boarders," she said simply, choosing not to ac-
knowledge his fear at the moment. "When people need to go
away, I keep their pets safe and healthy for them."

They left the room, and Noah's pulse began to return to
normal.

"Billie the Goat has a stall in the back" she said, filling a
bucket with food from a giant bin in the hall. "She generally
has free run of the property, but she sleeps back here."

She opened the last door with a snap, and instantly the head
of spiky white hair that would be the object of his nightmares
appeared in front of them.

Man and goat eyed each other. Man blinked first. Neither
moved.

"There you go, Ms. Goat," Hope said cheerfully, dumping
the entire bucket of food into Billie's trough, then filling her
water dish. "Say hello to Noah."

Billie almost looked as if she were smiling. Could goats
smile?

Noah swallowed hard.

"I'm getting the feeling you don't care for good ol' Billie
too much, Mr. Brandywine," Hope said, laughing at his expression.

"Let it suffice to say I'm wary. Why is she looking at me
like that?"

"Probably has a crush on you. She's very particular. You
should be flattered."

"I'll take that under consideration."

He couldn't help smiling. He also couldn't help feeling relieved when Hope had tucked the hairy creature in for the
night and closed the door so he couldn't see the big yearning
eyes. The odiferous thing petrified him.

Hope entered one more room in the back of the clinic.

"Aha!" he heard her say softly. "Is it time, Georgia?"

He peeked around her from the doorway. There was a huge pet bed on the floor in the center of the room. Lying upon it was the most gigantic dog Noah had ever seen. His pulse began hammering, and he was sure that the rhythmic beat of it could be heard across the room.

"That's a *dog?*" he exclaimed.

"A very special dog. That's Georgia, Mr. McShane's prize Great Dane. Mr. McShane had to go into the hospital for a heart catheterization this week, and Georgia's due, so I took her in. She could use some help anyway, as the litter is going to be so big."

The dog was looking longingly at Hope, very still, panting laboriously.

"Looks like it's time," she said excitedly.

"Time?" he said blankly. "Time for what?"

"For the puppies to arrive. She's whelping . . . she's in labor."

"Oh Geez," he said, backing slowly out of the room, his pulse picking up its pace to an even higher crescendo.

Hope turned and looked at him quizzically. He was tall and good looking. He could masterfully control a press conference. He was the president and owner of a worldwide corporation. He exuded a masculine power that could make her knees weak if she let it. But he was going to crumble at the thought of a puppy delivery. For some strange reason, the contrast was very appealing.

She rose to her feet just as his knees began to buckle. Without a second's hesitation, she put her arms firmly around his waist, pulling him to her, supporting him, resting her cheek on the lapel of his well-pressed suit. She could smell the appealing scent of his aftershave, the clean starchy smell of his white shirt. His arms tightened automatically around her, and his head bent down to ruffle the top of her head. He regained his balance, but he didn't let go.

"Oh, man, thanks," he said humbly, painfully aware that he had almost passed out. What would she think of him? What would she think of the man who stood a whole head taller than herself, who was struck down with fear at the sight of an animal? Shame and embarrassment flooded through him.

Somehow she had moved him out into the hallway. He didn't want to end the embrace, didn't want to meet her eyes and see the contempt he was sure would be there.

She made the decision for him. Gently, she positioned him in front of one of the chairs in the hallway.

"Sit down," she whispered, then pulled another chair to face him. They sat.

He met her eyes. Startled, he saw no contempt there, no laughter, no delight in his pain. He saw . . . compassion.

"Noah, what ever happened to make you so fearful of animals?" Her voice was feathery soft, her hands lay gently on his as she faced him.

The night was quiet around them, her touch was soothing and calm.

"When I was a little kid, my mom and I lived in this rusted old trailer outside of town. I grew up hearing horror stories about disease-ridden rats from the junkyard next door."

"No pets? No cat? No dog?" she asked gently.

He groaned. "No pets. But I had a run-in with the dog that patrolled the junkyard—ending with thirty-two stitches in my arm, and a series of horrific rabies shots in my stomach at the emergency ward."

She shook her head. "That's a nightmare. No wonder you think of animals in such a negative way."

No laughter, no recriminations. Her hand was still stroking his as she spoke, and his anxiety had disappeared. However, another startling emotion had taken its place. He watched her small hand move over his and felt a pang of emotion that was both unfamiliar and unexpected. What was this feeling?

But suddenly, a groan came from the giant dog in the room off the hall, and Hope jumped to her feet.

"You're okay?" she asked quietly. "I have to help Georgia. Duty calls. But rest as long as you like, and just shut the door on the way out. I'll be hours here."

Without another sound, she disappeared into the nearby

room, and he heard her soothing, calming tones as she reassured the dog in labor.

Noah was mesmerized, listening.

"That's it, girl. Go with it. Good doggie. Good Georgia. I'm right here, girl. It's okay. . . ."

He could hear the dog's even panting, mingled with her soft tones. Suddenly there was quiet.

Noah stood and walked to the door, unable to bear the suspense of wondering what was happening in the small room beyond his sight. He looked in.

"That's it. You're doing it. Good Doggie." The dog was silently straining, pushing, and with a sudden "whoosh," Hope assisted a tiny wet package into the world. Noah watched as she deftly broke the sac surrounding the tiny puppy and placed it near its mother's waiting mouth. Tiny squeals filled the air as Georgia proudly cleaned her first small pup, then prompted it toward its first meal.

Noah felt his throat tighten at the touching sight. Hope felt, rather than heard, his presence. She turned and looked at him, tears shining in her bright eyes.

"It never ceases to amaze me," she said softly. "The miracle of life."

He nodded, not trusting his voice.

Georgia groaned again. Hope sighed. "Okay, girl, here we go again." She smiled at Noah. "I think we're going to have quite a few little miracles of life before we get done here!"

Pup number two made its appearance, rapidly followed by pups three, four, and five. Hope repeated the routine over and over, the new puppies scrambling with each other as their number grew. Numbers six, seven, eight and nine arrived. Seeing the difficulty Hope was having handling both the tired mother and the endless line of puppies, he squatted down beside her and began assisting with the drying and placing of puppies.

Don't be afraid, he ordered himself. They are tiny, helpless puppies.

Georgia raised her tired head and looked at him suspiciously, and his heart almost stopped in his chest.

"It's okay, Georgia," Hope assured. "We can use the help here!" Georgia gave him a glance that seemed almost thankful. Hope flashed him a thousand-watt smile, and he felt a warm glow.

She handed him a sturdy box lined with clean towels. "Take the ones that are fed and dry, and collect them in this box. They'll keep each other warm, and it'll give Georgia more room."

Number ten arrived, followed quickly by number eleven. Hope palpitated the dog's stomach, looking concerned.

"Is something wrong? Is she done?"

"Can't help but think there's another one, but it seems like her contractions have stopped." She stroked the large dog softly.

"Come on, girl, give one more push."

The dog complied, astonishing him, and a final pup was born.

Hope looked at it sadly. "I don't think this one is breathing," she said, massaging it with a towel. "I think we may have lost her."

The pup was smaller than the rest, and Noah was horrified to find his eyes filling with tears.

"But isn't there something you can do?" His face looked stricken.

"Nature has its own selection, Noah. Sometimes it's out of our control. But we're not giving up yet. Here," she said, thrusting the small brown body wrapped in the towel at him. "Keep massaging her like this, while I take care of Georgia."

He massaged. And massaged. Hope settled the rest of the pups and assisted cleaning up Georgia so that she was able to take over her litter.

Out of the corner of her eye, she watched the multimillionaire as he sat on the tile floor of her clinic, his dark hair falling over his eyes as he bent his head to concentrate on the tiny patient.

Don't get carried away, she chided herself. *This is the same guy who tried to discredit you on national TV!*

"Come on, Baby, you can do it. You can do it. Take a breath, Baby. Live. Live."

His voice was low and comforting, a whole other dimension of the man she knew as Noah Brandywine. Her heart contracted as she watched the touching scene. Would the pup live?

Almost on cue, a tiny squeal pierced the air, and the pup in his hands began to wiggle.

"She's alive, she's alive!" he hollered, jumping up and holding the tiny pup in the air over his head. Hope began to laugh.

But Georgia was not so easily reassured. The giant dog leaped to her tired feet, feeling that her last pup was being threatened. On all fours, the Great Dane's head was higher than Noah's waist, which was scary enough. But standing on her back haunches, front paws on Noah's startled shoulders, she was eye to eye. And growling, teeth bared, eyes flashing.

Hope reacted quickly.

"Down, Georgia," she said quietly but forcefully, coaxing the upset dog off Noah's shoulders. "Now down, Noah," Hope instructed quickly, reaching to retrieve the pup as he brought his arms down. "Back down on the floor where you sat."

Noah didn't like the idea at all, but he followed directions. His pulse was racing and the flash of fear had made him break out in an immediate sweat. White-faced, he sat, so his head was lower than the dog.

Georgia's growling stopped immediately.

Crisis over, the giant dog turned her attention to her newest pup, ignoring Noah completely.

"It's ok. You just set off her mother instincts. She's okay now. Mothers can go to any extreme to protect their young."

His pulse was still pounding from his flash of fear, but he knew that her words were true. He had a sudden memory of his own mother.

"My mom was like that—sick and tired and trying to raise me in poverty, still fighting to her dying breath to do her best for me. She died when I was ten." What was he doing, pouring his heart out to this woman who had nearly brought his business to a grinding halt with her absurd accusations?

But Hope reached over and touched his arm gently. "I'm sure she'd be very proud of you right now."

He squared his shoulders, and Noah-the-Corporate-President was back. "She'd be very proud of all I've done with Brandywine Beauty," he said stiffly.

Hope laughed, and got to her feet. She signaled Noah to get up. Georgia rested peacefully with her new pups, and they left her quietly, shutting the clinic doors behind them as they stepped into the night air.

"Personally," Hope said, "I'm prouder of what you did for that pup."

Noah smiled, watching the moonlight reflect from the shiny bumper of his Jaguar. "Yeah," he conceded, "that was pretty amazing."

"Thanks for your help. That was a large litter. I don't think I could have done it on my own. Especially number twelve."

"The miracle of birth . . . it was good to see it—even if I did almost black out at the start."

He bent then, and placed a soft kiss on her mouth, without even thinking about it, as if it were the most natural thing in the world. Her lips were soft and warm. She pulled back, startled and blushing, one hand moving to the spot his mouth had kissed.

"Good night," she said softly, turning quickly and heading for her apartment door. She had left the boots at the clinic door, and was barefoot, still wearing her outrageous outfit.

"Hey Hope," he called as he stepped into the Jaguar. "Aren't you going to tell me where you were in that getup you're wearing?"

"Not on your life, Buster." She laughed, did a little dance on her bare toes, and then darted in the door.

He sat listening to the echo of her laugh in the dark night, before gliding the Jaguar into gear, and roaring off into the night.

* * *

A hot shower washed away the remnants of her disguise, and when she stepped from the shower she was mousse free, makeup free, and dirt free. The fake fingernails were long gone, littering the factory floor during her recent debacle. Visually, she guessed she looked like the old Hope Highfield who usually stared back at her in the mirror. But the night had changed things.

She hadn't proven a thing, except that Dirtbusters was probably not the culprit company involved in the cruel animal testing, and that she could absolutely make a total fool of herself in nothing flat.

Her fingers brushed her lips where his mouth had so unexpectedly met hers. A kiss. She licked her lips, feeling like a naughty child. But she had to admit it. She liked it. His kiss had melted her—almost.

And she had been standing there in her dirty bare feet with her scraped knees wobbling, her hair in stiff tangles, her makeup smudged under her eyes making her look like a contestant in a raccoon contest. Gorgeous? Ridiculous. She swallowed hard.

He was probably laughing at her, the magnificent wunderkind of the world of manufacturing. The giant of grooming, the magnate of makeup, the beauty bureaucrat had kissed her. By now he was probably ensconced in his upscale chrome and glass condo (and she had no doubt that it would be chrome and glass, to match the monstrosity he had built across her idyllic river) with a snifter of expensive brandy in his hand, leaning on the fireplace mantle (gas fireplace, of course, no smoke, no dirt, no mess) and telling humorous anecdotes about the psychotic little vet who had dared to question his ethics. And who would be hearing these anecdotes?

Her troubled imagination continued its flight. The listener would be blonde, and curvaceous, and sexy as anything, sprawled luxuriously on his sofa. Her makeup would be flawless. Her eyebrows would be properly tweezed. Not a zit in sight. Her dress would be from a designer line, made expressly for her.

Oh, Noah, she would croon with big adoring eyes, *what a*

quaint and silly little woman she must be. What a funny story. You must have died!

Pathetic, he would agree. *And you should have seen the shape of her nails. And that hair! I felt so bad for the poor thing, I actually kissed her!*

Hope actually growled at herself, bringing her wandering mind back to reality. It had just been a kiss. She had been surprised. She had been touched by his apparent enthusiasm over the puppies, when she knew he had overcome some internal fears. It had been a warm moment, that was all. She certainly wasn't going to stay up all night and worry about it.

She wasn't his type. But then, he wasn't hers either. In fact, he was everything she had gone to great lengths to avoid in her life. He was shallow, controlling, manipulative, self-satisfied, and unfriendly. The fact that he was a good kisser could not outweigh those characteristics, even if she had wanted them to—which she didn't. Not by a long shot.

She touched her lips again. *It's probably because it's a full moon,* she thought. *I'll feel better about this tomorrow.*

As Noah had put the Jag into gear, carefully navigating the bumpy driveway from Hope's Haven to the road, his feelings were as gnarled up as an unraveled ball of yarn. It had been a heck of a day. He'd spent thousands and thousands on damage control, getting good press, and getting his distribution system reestablished to keep his products rolling. He had given production bonuses, agreed to be guest speaker at ten additional national functions in the next two months to ingratiate himself with union leaders, health institutions, and city governments.

He'd worked his tail off, and then had ended up in the driveway of the big-mouthed pipsqueak who had started it all. To be fair, she didn't cause the problem. He himself had felt bad when he had seen those poor injured baby animals. Those animals didn't deserve it. (Except for that blasted goat. He wouldn't blame anybody who wanted to experiment on that stubborn bugger.) Someone was up to shenanigans, he agreed. But it wasn't him, and he was the one who had had to pay.

He banged the steering wheel at the thought, and then missed seeing a pothole, hearing the clunk of his tire as it bounced in and out. A mine field! Her darn driveway could be useful in time of war!

He pulled out onto the highway, thinking resignedly about the new realignment he would have to get for the Jag. Or maybe he should get a jeep, with four wheel drive and a suspension that lives forever, if he was going to traverse this ridiculous obstacle course that she called a driveway often. Which, of course, he wasn't. She had given it her best shot to bring him down, and she had failed. He had prevailed. Brandywine Beauty Products was up and running again.

He had no need to tangle with her again. And tangle was the word. He thought, suddenly, of how she had looked, sitting there with that big mean dog and all those little puppies. She had been so gentle, so understanding. He smiled at the thought. With her hair hanging down like it had just gone through a blender, and that makeup smeared on her face, she had still managed to be kind and caring. Real.

It had been a good experience, seeing those pups born, and saving that little one. He shuddered. He had always been so afraid of animals. But it was good to face your fears and wipe them out, like he had tonight.

He thought of the goat, and shuddered.

Well maybe the fears aren't totally wiped out, but I've made progress, he thought, consoling himself.

It wouldn't hurt to have a little more exposure to the animals, if just to tackle his fears and put them to rest. She had thanked him for helping with the pup. She had been kind and understanding about his panic over the animals, even if she was a bit weird. But he had never thanked her. He glanced at his watch. It wasn't even late. He could go back, right now, and thank her. She'd still be awake, he was sure. He turned the Jag around smoothly and headed back toward the battlefield of a driveway.

I'll only stay a minute, he told himself logically. *And it has nothing to do with the kiss. Nothing at all.*

The Jag bounced on a rock that materialized in front of him, and he let out a curse. *Yes, a jeep would come in handy.*

He was at the door again. Hope pulled the belt of her pink bathrobe tighter, and stared at him through the ancient screen door. Her hair was still wet, and again, her feet were bare. Was this some kind of a joke the gods were playing on her, that this handsome and aggravating man would only see her when she was either covered with mud or cat hair, or naked except for her bathrobe?

"You're back," she said, stating the obvious because she was at a loss for any meaningful words to say.

"I'm back," he answered, and then stood silently.

They stared at each other.

Finally, Hope burst out laughing.

"Okay, okay, I'm not sure what's going on here, Mr. Brandywine. What can I help you with?"

"I wanted to say thanks. For understanding about my panic with the animals. It's pretty embarrassing, you know. I'm not afraid of too much."

How well she knew that. She had seen his poised charm face angry news crews and nationwide TV without blinking an eye. He had the emotional courage of a lion.

"But I've always been afraid of animals. I felt like I learned something tonight, and I wanted to say thanks. That's all."

Hope was touched.

"Would you like to come in, maybe have a cup of tea?" As soon as she said the words, she wanted to take them back. She remembered the bathrobe, her hair, and her vision of his beautiful fawning blonde waiting for him at home.

"I'd love it." He stepped inside.

"Well, sit a minute," she said, pointing to the couch. "I'll put some clothes on." She darted to the bedroom and pulled on a pair of jeans and a clean sweatshirt. Not exactly like his golden girls, but realistic and honest. She wouldn't allow herself to be ashamed of her casual style. What you see is what you get. She had fought a hard battle to be her own person, and she wasn't going to let any insecurities make her feel bad about herself.

She was running a brush through her tangled hair when she heard the noise, a rather strangled cry coming from the living room.

"Arrghhh! Oomyygosshhhhh!" Noah was croaking.

She dropped the brush and sped to the living room.

When she saw him, sitting on the couch, frozen to the spot, her eyes opened wide.

There was a parrot sitting on top of his head.

Chapter Four

Hope didn't know whether to laugh or cry at the sight. She crossed the room quickly, and arched a finger at the precariously perched bird.

"Very funny, Penelope," she chided, her arm extended, and stoically trying to keep a straight face.

"Very funny, Penelope," echoed the bird, making a little effortless jump over to her finger. She walked the bird across the room to a tall cage that took up the corner of the room, and ushered the parrot inside. The cage door shut with a click.

Noah began breathing again.

"I'm really sorry," she said. "I forgot. I let the bird wander when I'm here alone. I never thought . . ."

"Your animals seem to think I'm a target of some kind," his voice was thick, embarrassed. There was sweat on his brow again. "I guess I shouldn't have come, but I wanted to thank you, and I hoped that if I had more exposure to animals . . ."

"You'd overcome your fear."

"Precisely." He said, his voice growing stronger. "But I don't think I'm ready for any more of these 'Close Encounters of the Furred Kind.' "

He was suspiciously eyeing a kitten that had stuck a paw out from under the chair near where he sat.

"Nope, definitely not ready." He stood and moved jerkily toward the door.

The kitten attacked his shoe, and he jumped. Hope bent down quickly and retrieved the kitten, putting it in the bedroom and closing the door.

"I guess that's a negative for the tea then," she said, watching him.

He nodded. "I'd rather face a nuclear missile than your wildlife supply, Dr. Highfield. I'd like to get used to animals, but in small doses. I mean, you have a lot of animals here— the dogs, the cats, the parrot, the rabbits, the goat. All you need is an alligator and a big snake, and you'd probably qualify as a zoo."

"There's a twelve-foot boa constrictor in a cage at the back of the hospital."

He paled. "I'm not surprised."

She stepped out the door with him. The night air was cool, the sky was clear.

"I'm sure if you put your mind to it, you'll do it."

She was being kind, he knew. The moonlight shone down, lighting her freshly scrubbed face, and suddenly he wasn't thinking about the animals anymore. He was thinking of the earlier kiss, and wanting to repeat it.

She was standing close, smelling faintly of soap. He put a finger under her chin and raised her head, and his lips came down upon hers, stealing her breath away, and making her legs turn to jelly. She leaned against him, savoring the feel of him, her mouth opening to his kiss as his tongue explored. She melted.

And then, literally in a flash, it was over. The eye-blinding glare of a high-intensity camera flashbulb exploded nearby. The shock of the sudden light brought them back to earth instantly.

"What the—" Noah exclaimed, spinning around toward the light.

A young man in a denim jacket and khaki pants stood nearby, baseball cap on his head, camera around his neck.

"Sorry to bother you, folks," he laughed, already turning on his heel. "But news is news!"

The reporter took off down the dark driveway in a run, with Noah right behind him.

"You creep," Hope heard him yell angrily as he chased the reporter, then heard his muffled cry as he stumbled into a pothole and went sprawling. Noah returned to the lighted driveway with a limp and a torn trouser leg.

"Are you all right?" she called out.

"Never better," he said in a monotone. "But I've got to get out of here, Hope. Good night." He reached his Jag, climbed in, and drove off into the night.

Hope watched his taillights disappear, then stepped back into the house, mind racing, legs still wobbly from his kiss.

How much more of this could she take?

"Very funny, Penelope," squawked the parrot from its cage.

"Watch yourself, my feathered friend, don't push me!" she said through gritted teeth, as she opened the cage and let the bird free.

"Watch yourself!" echoed the bird, flitting up to the curtainrod.

"Good advice," she grumbled, and went to bed.

"Yo, Doc! Wake up!"

There was a persistent pounding on the door, and Hope pulled the blankets over her head, hoping that the sound would go away.

"Wake up, Doc!" Manny's loud voice infiltrated her fog of sleep. "I can't wait to hear what I missed last night. You're a celebrity, that's all there is to it. Come on, get up and spill the goods!"

Hope untangled herself from the covers and practically fell out of bed. It had taken her hours to fall asleep, and then morning had come way too fast. She pulled on her jeans and sweatshirt and went to let Manny in.

"Why are you torturing me?" she complained as she opened the door. "It's Saturday morning. People like to sleep in on the weekend, haven't you heard that?"

Manny laughed and poked a paper cup of steaming hot coffee toward her. "Here, I come bearing gifts."

She gratefully took the coffee, and sipped it right away.

"And here," he added, handing her the newspaper. "I come bearing news."

She took the paper from him absentmindedly and unfolded it, glancing down at the headline. She screamed.

"I don't believe it! Of all the nerve!" Staring back at her was a two-inch headline, "*Make Up, Make Over or Make Out?*" And right beneath the headline was a six-by-ten photo in living color—of Dr. Hope Highfield and Noah Brandywine, with their lips locked together in a passionate kiss.

"I knew I was going to miss something good if I left last night," Manny howled. "You're smooching! And for the press! And I thought you didn't even *like* the guy!"

"Manny, this isn't funny," she said in a low voice.

"Funny? It gives new meaning to funny. Who would have thunk it, Dr. Hope losing her head over the Makeup Man?"

"I did *not* lose my head."

"Now maybe I'm just speculating, Dr. Hope, but did you lose anything else too? I'm noticing those ain't the same clothes I left you in after your escapade."

She picked up a couch pillow and flung it at him, making him jostle his own cup of coffee, making it spill. "Don't say ain't."

"Ow, ow, hot, hot," he said, doing a jig as the hot black liquid spilled on his wrist. "Take it easy, Doc. I'm sure there's a good explanation. Like it was another one of your amazing plans, right? To get him to confess? The kiss torture technique?"

Manny couldn't stop laughing. Hope couldn't stop fuming.

"It was a mistake, a stupid mistake. And all of a sudden there was a reporter there, and the flash went off."

She plopped onto the sofa. "I could just die of embarrassment."

Manny sat beside her. "Oh, don't get so worked up. Maybe everybody here turns to the sports page first. And it doesn't even look much like you. Maybe no one will even notice it."

The phone rang.

"Hi, Mr. Strand, how's your dog Buffy?" she said into the phone when she answered it. "Yes, I did see the picture."

She listened.

"Yes, I was wearing that sweatshirt you brought me from the shore. Yes, it does look nice. Thank you for calling."

The phone rang again.

"Hello, Mrs. Wilson. How's your cat Mildred? What?" She made a desperate face at Manny. "Yes, he's quite tall. Like your dear departed husband? That's nice, dear. Thank you for calling."

The phone wouldn't stop.

"No, Mrs. Wendell, there are no wedding plans. I promise you would be the first to know."

"Hello Melvin. Yes, I saw the paper. No, I do not want his name tattooed on my buttocks. But thanks for asking. How's Percival? Pregnant again? Melvin, this is too many kittens, we are going to have to talk about this on your next visit."

"The Daily Tattler? No, I do not want to do an interview about an affair with Mr. Brandywine. There is no affair. It was really just a little friendly kiss. Please leave me alone."

After the first round of calls, Manny took over answering the phone and she escaped to the office to begin her vet appointments, and to avoid hearing Manny's avid conversations about her infamous pose.

But almost every client had something to say all morning.

"It's about time, my dear. We've been a little worried that you'd be left an old maid," said the well-meaning elderly O'Connell sisters.

"Well, if you don't want him, give him my number," said

the buxom blonde cocktail waitress, Melissa, after getting shots for her cat.

Mr. and Mrs. Bradford patted her hand when they came in to pick up horse liniment for their aging pony. "Just be sure he doesn't break your heart, Dr. Hope. Emma here says she's read in the society pages that he's quite a rake. Just be careful."

When they were leaving, they handed her a basket of fresh eggs, their payment for the medicine. "But if he's not a rake, perhaps you could make him a nice omelet sometime soon."

Hope smiled, and nodded, and tried to keep things in perspective during her office hours, even though she felt like crying.

They say a picture is worth a thousand words. Well, she'd like to say a thousand words or so to that sneaky photographer if she could get her hands on him!

When Noah had returned home that night, there had been no sexy blonde draped across his sofa as there had been in Hope's vibrant imagination. However, at the crack of dawn, there was a furious one at his front door, whacking the doorbell as with a vengeance.

He answered the door in his knee-length robe, a mug of steaming coffee in his hand.

"Cheryl!" he exclaimed, running a hand across his tired face, feeling the razor stubble and knowing that he probably looked horrible. He had had a terrible night. "I didn't know you were coming. But come in, come in."

If he had been more awake, he would have picked up on the angry look that flashed in her eyes.

She strode angrily past him, thrusting a folded newspaper into his stomach as she crossed the room, depositing herself in his best leather chair, and crossing her legs expectantly.

"Well?" she said sarcastically. "I'm ready to hear your explanation."

He looked at her, seeing rage pouring from every perfect pore, and he was baffled for a moment. They had been dating for several months, but he had never seen her like this.

Had he forgotten her birthday? To the best of his knowledge, she didn't celebrate those, preferring to stay twenty-nine forever. A holiday? Nothing came to mind. Had they had plans? If they had, it had honestly skipped his mind. He hadn't even spoken to her since—well, for two days, since the letter had appeared in the paper, turning his business upside down.

To tell the truth (which he wasn't about to), he hadn't even given her a thought. He felt a flash of guilt, deciding this was the cause of her anger.

"I'm sorry, Cheryl. I should have called you. If you've seen the paper, you've seen that I've been having major business problems, and they've been taking up all my time. Pickets all over the place. Distribution all but cut off for the better part of a day. Cost me an arm and a leg to get things straight again."

Cheryl squinted her eyes at him, and pursed her perfect lips.

Candy Cotton Pink, his mind registered. She was wearing one of the new spring lipstick shades from Bradywine Beauty.

"Work just took all your time? Fighting off pickets? But you've got your distribution back on track?"

He nodded, watching her cautiously. "What's the matter, Cheryl? You know that I take my business very seriously. Sometimes I have to give it 100 percent."

"Take a look at the front page, Mr. 100 percent. What exactly were you distributing there?"

He opened the paper, and the picture of him kissing Hope Highfield leapt out at him. His jaw dropped.

"And just who, may I ask, is that?" Cheryl asked frostily. "And do you have any idea how humiliating it is for me to have you plastered over the front page with some local trollop? Why, look at that hair! She looks like she just got out of the shower."

Noah stared at her, and then back at the picture, noticing the fine line of Hope's chin, and the way her head was tucked into his shoulder. Like it fit. He smiled at the thought.

"She's not a trollop. Her name is Hope. And she *had* just gotten out of the shower." He remembered the fresh clean smell of soap, and the clearness of her freshly scrubbed skin. "I'm sorry if the picture upset you, Cheryl."

But as he read the headline, "Make Up, Make Over, or Make Out?" all he could think of was Hope's reaction. She'd be fit to be tied.

"She's the veterinarian who's been up in arms about people experimenting on animals. She thought Brandywine Beauty was involved in it."

"And so what if you were? Business is business. But why are you *kissing* her, Noah? This is so absurd."

"I'd never be involved in testing on animals, Cheryl. It's cruel and unnecessary."

Cheryl stood. "Whatever." She looked bored.

"Cheryl, have you ever had a pet?" he asked.

She wrinkled her powdered nose. "Whatever for? They stink, they make a mess, and they need so much care. My housekeeper would never forgive me. Listen, I'm out of here. I'm going to consider if I can forgive you for this—indiscretion, Noah Brandywine. But you'd better come up with a nice present. Go shave now. You certainly need it. Call me tonight."

She crossed the room toward the door, kissing the air next to his cheek as she passed. She would not dare to smear her perfect makeup.

The door shut behind her and she was gone, leaving behind a faint trace of Passion Flower, an exclusive Brandywine scent.

He stared after her, horrified at his reaction to her words, her thoughts, her values. Had he never really listened to her before?

And then he thought of Hope in her big boots, dragging creatures from the river to save them. A housekeeper? Hope needed a zookeeper. He laughed out loud at the thought. It had been a long time since he had laughed like that.

And then he was speeding to the shower, to shave and to dress. He pulled a sweat suit out of a drawer, and his sneakers from the closet. It was his only casual clothing, reserved for workouts at the athletic club. But what exactly did one wear when one was going to run into a goat?

He was going to see Hope.

The phone rang. Frank Johnson's gravelly voice came over the line. "Everything's flowing A-okay now, Boss, and the tree-hugging animal lovers have stopped picketing. But this crap in the paper—this picture—what were you thinking? What are you doing with this troublemaking broad?"

"She's not a troublemaking broad, Frank. She's a little eccentric, maybe. A little too principled. But she believed what she said at the time."

"And now? You think she's done? Are you fooling yourself, Noah? This one's got trouble written all over her. She's obviously on a mission to ruin you. Besides the fact that she isn't even your type. You oughta stay away from her. Far away. Don't let her set you up again."

"Set me up? Now who's being imaginative? She didn't have anything to do with the photographer. She was as upset as I was."

"Sure. Whatever you say. But don't go losing your edge, Noah. You know how to watch your back. We oughta know all we can about this one. I've just got a feeling—"

"Listen, Frank, we were wrong in that deal about her father. I don't want to go off the deep end again. Let it go. Don't bother her. This will all pass over. She's really quite enchanting, in an aggravating kind of way. But thanks for cleaning up the mess and getting this running smoothly again. I appreciate it."

"That's what you pay me so well to do, Buddy. What time are you coming into the office? Any meetings scheduled?"

"Nothing scheduled that I know of. But to tell you the truth, since it's Saturday and there are no fires to put out, I thought I'd take the day off."

There was a moment of silence.

"A day off?" Frank asked quizzically. He had never heard those words from Noah Brandywine in his ten years as his security specialist.

"A day off. A couple of personal things to attend to. But I'll put in a few hours tomorrow to get ready to hit the week running on Monday."

"Okay." Frank answered thoughtfully. "And would any of these personal things have to do with the mysterious Dr. Highfield?"

Noah actually laughed. "I'll never tell. I'll see you Sunday."

There was more going on here than met the eye. Frank Johnson prided himself on being an excellent judge of human nature, and Noah Brandywine was not acting according to form.

He glanced down at the paper on his desk, the picture of Noah and Hope glaring up at him. Two days ago, they had never even heard of Hope Highfield. But she had appeared, and for some reason, life had been upside down since. He decided that he had better find out as much about her as he could. It would be in Noah's best interest to face the facts about this elfish little woman with the big eyes who seemed to have thrown him for a loop.

Within minutes, Noah was on his way to Hope's Haven, to do whatever it took to make up to Hope Highfield for having her name and picture smeared all over the press.

It was easier to traverse the drive in the daylight, and also easier to see the conglomeration of ruts and weeds and rough stones.

How could anyone have a driveway like that? he thought in amazement.

He parked the car, noticing that Hope's aged Suburban wagon was not in its usual place. He saw the wobbly bicycle of her assistant parked beneath the tree by the door of the clinic.

Gingerly, he walked to the clinic door, with his eyes doing constant surveillance for wandering wildlife. Not a single creature accosted him.

"Hi," he said through the screen door, seeing Manny perched on top of the desk, with a box holding kittens in his lap. He was feeding them with an eyedropper. Music played in the background.

"Very good, very good," he crooned to the little black kitten in his palm. "You are going to get big and strong. You will see. Good!" He looked up and saw Noah, and his eyes lit with curiosity. "Ah, Mr. Brandywine, come in, come in."

He noticed the sweat clothes.

"I almost didn't recognize you without your designer duds." Noah smiled.

"Sorry to bother you. I came to see Dr. Highfield."

"You don't bother me, except don't mind that I don't stop what I'm doing. Once I have these critters on a roll, I just want to keep going. They don't like to eat too much."

Noah stepped in the room and looked into the box. Little baby kittens were huddled in a ball, sleeping, while Manny fed one. All of the kittens had shaved spots on their backs.

"Oh boy," said Noah, feeling sick, "Are those more of the animals that were used for testing? They're so little."

"Isn't it disgusting? I pulled them out of the river this morning. Also several rabbits and a few guinea pigs. The pigs didn't make it, but we're making progress with these."

"It's such a shame. I'm really sorry."

"You got anything to be sorry about, Mr. Brandywine?" The youth's black eyes flashed.

"No, no, that's not what I meant. Don't start that again. I don't have anything to do with it. But I'm sorry that it's happening, just the same."

"Yeah, well. We'll get to the bottom of it yet. And I feel sorry for the creeps, when the doc gets her hands on them."

"Speaking of the doc. Is she here?"

"Nope, the doc ain't here. Isn't here," he corrected himself. "Went to the Wests' farm, right after her morning office hours. Their cow is dropping a calf, but it's breach, so the doc went to help."

"A breach?"

"The calf is facing the wrong way, and the old cow can't deliver it. All the arms and legs get tangled up, it's a heck of a mess. Hope has to straighten things out."

"Straighten them out? How does she do that?" All of a sudden, Manny thought the makeup man was looking a little green around the gills.

"She has to reach in and—" He was definitely looking green now, a bright shade of green. "Never mind. She just fixes things, that's all. But I'll tell her you came over. She'll be hours."

Noah's face was losing its unsightly hue.

"I wanted to talk to her about the picture in the paper."

"I'll bet."

"I guess she saw it."

"In Technicolor."

"I guess she was embarrassed."

"Good guesser."

"Maybe people didn't see it."

"Maybe the Pope's not Polish."

Noah frowned and ran a hand over his face. "Well, I wanted to apologize."

Manny's voice got hard. "You sorry for that, too, Mr. Brandywine? You have anything to do with that photographer, or are you just sorry it happened, like the animal torturing?"

"Don't push me, kid," Noah said evenly. "You know what I mean. I didn't do anything to hurt those animals, and I would never do anything to hurt Hope Highfield. Ever."

Manny laid the kittens down then, and stood, looking directly into Noah's eyes.

"Maybe you already have. Hope is not the type to go around kissing every Tom, Dick and. . . . Noah. According to the press, you are not nearly as selective. Don't hurt her, man, 'cause you won't get the chance to hurt her twice." The dark eyes didn't blink.

Noah peered back at him thoughtfully. It was one thing to feel anger at a young punk who dared to call him on the carpet. It was another to realize that he had a grudging respect for the principled kid who reminded him more than a little of his earlier self. He was glad that Hope had a comrade like that.

"Message received," he said calmly. "Tell Hope I was here.

I'll find something to do to pay her back for her embarrassment."

A cat sprung up onto the desk, trying to investigate the kittens in the box. Noah jumped.

"I know you're not comfortable with the animals," Manny said, a worried look on his face. "But you got to realize the animals are Hope's life."

"I'll learn. I'll adjust. And meanwhile," he reached into his pocket and plucked two hundred dollar bills out of his bulging money clip, "use this to feed those injured animals for a spell."

Manny's eyes opened wide at the sight of the money.

"Man," he whistled softly, holding the money up to the light. "This'll buy a pile of cat food. She really could use some cash money around here. You sure you want to do this, Mister?"

"Sure," said Noah. "It's even tax deductible. See you later, kid."

He was halfway down the driveway when he got his next brilliant idea. He dialed the phone and Frank answered on the first ring. "You know that guy we hired to do the driveways at the plant last year? I want you to call him, and get him to deliver a few loads of crushed stone."

He gave the details to an astonished Frank. The job would be done promptly, Noah knew, even if Frank was sure he was nuts.

Noah was whistling as he pulled the Jag into the parking lot of the park on the edge of town. It was time to meet his fears head on.

He took a spot in the far corner of the lot, parking the Jag on a diagonal in two spaces to protect it from scratches. He set the automatic locks and crossed the grass to the walking path that began right in front of his car.

The sun was bright, and the park felt like a happy place. Just right for his plan. If he was going to adjust to animals with success, he was going to have to do it one at a time, instead of immersing himself in the conglomeration at Hope's Haven. Slow but sure. Step by step.

His step felt light in his sneakers as he moved quickly along the path, surveying the park. Lots of people walked dogs here. Nice, safe dogs on nice, safe leashes. He spotted an elderly man walking a poodle coming toward him.

"Excuse me, sir," Noah said. "That's a nice dog you have there."

"Thank you," the man said curtly, walking past without stopping.

Deterred but not defeated, Noah walked on.

He approached the next pet walker with a confident air. "Nice dog, Ma'am," he said cheerily. "May I pet him?"

"Only if you want to lose a hand, buddy," the young woman said matter of factly, as the dog bared his teeth and took an aggressive stance. "He's trained to protect me from strangers."

Noah stepped back. Way back. "And a wonderful job he does of it, if I may say so," he said, rapidly lengthening the distance between him and the sharp white teeth. This was not proving to be an easy task.

As the morning wore on, the number of pet walkers diminished. Noah sat on a park bench, shoulders slumped, deep in thought. A gentle nudging on his knee brought him back to the present. There was a hairy creature sitting on the ground, next to him, looking at him expectantly. It was a dog—or so he thought. But if he had to name the breed, he would be hard pressed. It was most likely a Heinz 57 variety. Long hair, definitely needing a brush. It was brownish, a little greyish, a little blackish. Whatever. It was about ninety-five pounds of hair, with dark eyes peeking out at him.

The dog was very still. Noah had been ignored, growled at (by both walkers and walkees), snarled at, and barked at all morning. As this particular dog was not making any of those aggressive moves toward him, Noah sat where he was and watched him. Interesting creature, this dog.

After a few moments of mutual staring, the dog, which Noah had already nicknamed "Hair," decided to take a nap and collapsed at Noah's feet. Within seconds, the dog's raucous snore filled the air. Noah looked around to see if anybody was watching.

Did dogs usually snore? He had no idea. The dog had bad

sinuses maybe, or perhaps a cold. It wasn't a bad sound, actually. It was almost comforting, a rhythmic rumble like clockwork.

Noah sat where he was, partly because he didn't really have anyplace else to go, and partly because he had ninety-five pounds of dog sitting on his feet.

He crossed his arms, put his head back, and closed his eyes, feeling the warmth of the sun on his face. Relaxed, he breathed in the fresh air of the park. Within seconds, he was sound asleep.

Some time later, there was another tapping on his knee. He opened his eyes abruptly, startled for a minute by the brightness of the sunlight. Where was he?

The dog awoke too, with a loud snort.

He focused on the figure standing in front of him. A blue uniform. A shiny badge. A nightstick. It was a cop.

"Hello, Officer." He tried to stand up, feeling at a disadvantage on the park bench, but the dog was still sitting on his feet.

"Sorry to bother you, Sir, but we have strict rules here."

The cheerful public servant was writing in a little notebook. He ripped off the top sheet and handed it to Noah.

"This is a ticket for not obeying the local ordinances as pertains to pets in the park. No leash. No collar. The fine is $100 for the first offense. I'm assuming this is your first offense?"

"Yes, I mean, no." He pushed the dog with his foot and stood up. "This isn't my dog, officer. There's no offense. This dog is a stray, that's all."

Hair had risen from his nap, refreshed, and now sat by Noah's right leg, leaning into him, and looking up at him with adoring eyes. He was panting.

"Really, sir. Lying isn't necessary. If you forgot the leash, you forgot the leash. It's obvious it's your dog."

"I don't have a dog. Seriously. I don't even like dogs." He pulled out his wallet, showing his license. "I'm sure we can straighten this out. I'm Noah Brandywine, the president of

Brandywine Beauty Products. I was just taking a walk in the park. By myself."

The officer looked at him strangely, then at the license, then at the dog.

"I believe I've seen you in the paper."

"That's right. Brandywine Beauty Products. Noah Brandywine." He stuck out his hand to shake hands with the officer. The officer didn't offer his hand in return.

"You're that one who hates animals, right? Some doctor is suing you?"

Noah blanched. "Absolutely not. There was some confusion, and Dr. Highfield questioned my testing techniques. It seems that someone is experimenting with animals, and she thought it was me. But it wasn't." He was stammering now. "It wasn't me. I'd never do such a thing."

"Because you love animals so much, Mr. Brandywine?"

The officer was looking down at the dog leaning on Noah's leg. He held out the ticket.

Noah sighed, taking the ticket and putting it into his pocket. He knew when he was licked.

"Because I love animals so much, officer."

The man shook his head, and turned to walk away. "Get a leash, Mr. Brandywine. The second fine is $200."

"Scat!" Noah grimaced in irritation at the hairy dog, as soon as the cop was out of sight. "Look what you've done! I didn't deserve this darn ticket!"

The dog gave him a sideways glance, and began to walk slowly off. Was the dog smirking? Could dogs smirk?

Noah turned the other way and began to jog. If he wasn't going to succeed in his obviously stupid animal quest, at least he could get some exercise. It would be a month of Sundays before he took a day off from work like this. What a waste of time!

After running about a mile, he slowed to pace himself. He crossed in front of a large tree, and noticed a little girl standing beneath the wide branches, looking up, and crying.

"What's the matter?" he asked kindly. There didn't seem to be any adults around.

"It's Muffin, my kitty," she wailed, stomping her little foot. "She climbed up the tree when a big dog ran by, and I can't get her down.

Noah looked up into the leafy expanse of branches. He couldn't see a thing, but he could hear the stranded kitten.

"Mew!" came a high-pitched feline cry from high up in the tree.

"My kitty! My kitty!" the little girl bawled, her blond hair swinging as her shoulders shook with life-sized sobs.

Noah glanced around in a panic. Wasn't there somebody able to help this kid? Where was her mother? Where was the dedicated cop? Where was Superman?

There was no one in sight but this tear-soaked little girl— and him.

He gave a sigh that came deep from his solar plexus. In business circles, he was known as a problem solver extraordinaire. He could create, instigate, and manipulate with the best of them. *But could he climb a tree?*

He wasn't going to let a little kitten get the best of him. Just because he had never done it *before,* didn't mean he couldn't manage it *now.*

"I'll get the kitten," he said bravely to the little girl. "So you can stop crying."

She nodded solemnly, and watched her hero climb the tree.

The lower branches were a snap, spaced far enough apart to give him room to maneuver, and all strong enough to hold his weight. He hoisted himself up to the next level, his head disappearing into the leafy greenery.

"Meow!" said the little kitten, who finally came into view. She was a little orange cat, looking a bit like a fluffy baby tiger, and she was perched well up into the tree branches.

Noah ignored the nagging little voice that chanted, "Uh oh!" in his head. Heroes didn't suffer this doubt, he was certain.

He climbed higher. So did the kitten.

"Stop climbing, cat," he whispered helplessly to the errant feline, as he pulled himself higher into the tree. Branches snagged at his sweatpants and poked him in the ear.

The higher he went, the closer together the branches grew,

leaving him little or no space to wiggle though. He had to test each branch with his foot, to be sure it would take his weight.

"Here kitty, kitty, kitty," called the little girl, not crying now, but still eager to see her pet.

He was getting closer. The kitten had stopped moving any higher, probably because it was running out of branches to climb.

Up here in the treetops, the wind blew slightly, making the branches sway. Noah felt slightly queasy. Did Superman have these problems?

The cat moved suddenly toward him, carefully placing each little paw on the next branch.

"Meow!" said Muffin as she moved face to face with Noah.

"Nice kitty!" he whispered, eye to eye with the cat. What was he going to do now? The rescue had not been a very well thought out plan! His pulse was hammering. The cat was unconcerned.

"Meow!" said Muffin, apparently at ease. She gently continued her delicate descent, one branch at a time, moving right past her would-be-but-paralyzed rescuer, as if she hadn't a care in the world.

He started breathing again, watching the little kitten's tail wiggle as she made her way down the tree. Crisis averted. The cat would be fine. He could get down now.

Except that he couldn't. He was stuck. His right sneaker was firmly wedged between the two highest branches that he had decided could hold his weight, and every movement that he made to pull his foot *up* to get loose was causing another problem.

The tree branches that poked him incessantly from behind had gotten caught in the waistband of his sweatpants, and when he tried to move either foot up, they were pulling his sweatpants down. If he wasn't careful, there would be a full moon in the park on this sunny day.

The kitten had climbed down to the lower branches, and he heard the little girl's delighted voice.

"Muffin, my Muffin," she cried as she pulled the little ball of fluff into her arms. "Thank you, Mister!" she called up to him.

"Mary? Mary?" came a female voice as a jogger approached the tree.

"Mommy!" the little girl called. "Muffin got stuck in the tree but that nice man shooed her down!"

"Thanks," the little girl's mother called up into the tree, as she guided the child away. "You should be careful talking to strangers," she added quietly to her daughter as they moved away.

Noah watched them leave from his eagle's eye perch in the tree. His career as a superhero was absolutely over. Not even a resumé item. He turned his efforts to freeing his foot (and his sweatpants) so he could return to the ground with some type of dignity.

The kitten had gotten herself down, and he would, too. *What goes up must come down*, he thought stoically, as he gave his foot a forceful tug.

The next thing he new, he was plummeting through the branches, arms and legs flapping, heading on a direct course with the ground. He landed with a thud, all possible air forced from his lungs. *What goes up must come down.* He grimaced. He was on his back, looking up into the bright blue sky. He was alive. He hurt all over. A dark shadow moved over him.

He shook his head and focused his gaze. A tousled brownish, blackish, greyish mop with eyes was hanging over him. Hair the dog sniffed, then lay down beside him and licked his face.

"That's it!" he yelled like a man possessed. "I've had it! I'm out of here!" He did his best to leap to his feet, though it was more like an uncomfortable climb.

"Not so fast!" came an authoritative and angry voice that was just a tad familiar.

Noah turned his stiff neck and saw the policeman approaching him. He held another citation in his hand.

"No climbing trees in this park. It's posted. It's absolutely forbidden. Are you just looking for trouble?"

"I was trying to save a kitten for a little girl, officer," he protested weakly. To the best of his knowledge, he didn't think Superman ever had to explain breaking a window or jaywalking in traffic to the local gendarmes on one of his superheroic quests.

"I don't see any kitten, or any little girl, either." He held out the citation, and Noah took it. This day was turning out to be downright humiliating.

"Any other rules this dog that I don't own and I should be made aware of?" he said sarcastically, as the dog rubbed himself against his leg, and then took off down the path.

"Don't be a wise guy," said the cop, walking away. "And pull your pants up, or I'll not only cite you, I'll have you arrested."

Belatedly, Noah noticed his sweatpants were halfway down from the fall. *Well, a half moon is better than a full moon*, he thought angrily. He yanked them up and started walking quickly toward his car. He was getting out of this park before anything else could happen.

He approached his car, which was all alone now in the corner of the near empty lot. Hair, the dog, was sitting on his front hood. He looked around wildly. Candid Camera? Funniest Home Videos? The Wrath of the Gods? No one was there. Except Hair, of course.

So what was he to do? He opened the door and the dog jumped in, settling into the passenger seat like it was his honored place. He opened the sun roof. The dog stuck his moppy head out. He headed the car for Hope's Haven, to give Hope the stray.

And then he was going to the chiropractor to straighten out his back. And maybe to the psychiatrist, to straighten out his head. Too many days like this, and he'd be headed for the funny farm, for sure!

Chapter Five

Could *a day get much worse than this?* Hope hung up the telephone and rotated her aching shoulders, rolling her neck from side to side. She ached all over. It had taken hours to deliver the Wests' calf, and it had also taken all the physical strength she could muster. She had almost lost them both, the straining mother and the defiant baby, who had seemed to fight so strongly against making an appearance in this world. She had twisted and pulled and maneuvered and rotated. And finally, she had succeeded.

That had been the good part of the day. She had felt the gratitude bestowed upon her by the grateful farmer and his young son who had stood by and watched, helping when they could. She had felt the gratitude of the exhausted mother as the calf was finally born. And she had seen the beauty of the spindly little calf as it unfolded its wobbly legs and balanced for the first time, suckling from his mother. Seeing life regenerated like this was beautiful.

But not without price. She was exhausted.

At the start of the day, with her tabloid-style photo on the front page of the paper, she had been upset. There sure must be a lack of any worthwhile news if a single kiss could generate such publicity! But she had faced the embarrassment, the ridiculous innuendos, the well-meaning cracks from her clients, her friends, and the world in general. Sooner or later, she would set them all straight.

The question is, she thought with instantly reddening cheeks at the memory of that ill-timed kiss, would she ever get her own emotions straight?

She had gotten through her office hours, and delivered the calf. But then the phone had rung.

"It's your father," whispered Manny as he had handed her the receiver.

"I have a copy of today's newspaper in my hand. I hope you are pleased with yourself, Hope Elizabeth Highfield," his voice had boomed. "Making yourself the laughingstock of the public world. What do you have to say for yourself?"

Her fingers tightened around the phone, turning white. She fought for composure. His critical words had always felt like weapons drawn against her, and she had worked hard for many years to be able to overcome their sting. She took a deep breath, centered herself.

"I'm pretty darn photogenic, wouldn't you say?" she retorted, her sarcasm her shield.

"What on earth were you thinking of?" he blasted her. "The Highfield name carries with it a banner of respectability, of honor—how dare you besmirch it this way? You should be ashamed of yourself."

She had heard it all before, though, of course, this was the first time the issue was her picture in the paper. She knew that many people would envy her childhood, growing up as the daughter of multi-millionaire Hugh Highfield in the affluent Philadelphia suburbs in a house that resembled a castle more than a family home. She had had everything that a person could desire. Except choice. Except freedom.

Everything in life comes with a pricetag, and being one of the heirs of the Highfield fortune was no exception. Her life had been controlled. The right schools, the right friends, the right social activities, the right clothes. All had been chosen for her with the utmost care. She had hated every minute of it.

There were four Highfield offspring; her older brother Brent, who had been revered for his leadership in the air force during the Afghanistan crisis, and who would eventually take her father's position at the head of the board of directors. There was her younger sister, Diana, who reveled in clothing and travel and all the society benefits that Highfield money could buy, following stalwartly in their mother's proper footsteps. And there was Prince, the baby of the family, still in college, and showing every indication of living up to the Highfield values of money and power.

She loved them all. But she was different. She had always been different. And while her siblings had eventually understood her choices, her father had not. When she had decided to pursue a career in veterinary medicine at the University of Pennsylvania, he had given her a final ultimation. "Do as I say or be disinherited."

She had chosen freedom. She had used every penny she could personally scrape together, had applied for loans and had worked two jobs while going to vet school full time. And she had never regretted it. She was proud of the life she had built for herself, the values she had decided to live by.

And through the years that followed, Hugh Highfield had shown that he had a grudging respect for his stubborn daughter. They had maintained a certain kind of relationship, and though it had been a little strained at times, they had learned to deal with each other.

But this had probably been possible because she had never crossed the boundary, had never done anything public that would cast any negative aspersions on the Highfield "honor" or the Highfield name. Until today, with her face plastered all over the paper.

"How could you let yourself be so used, Hope Elizabeth? Can't you see that this man has maneuvered you into looking like a fool in the press? You dared to attack his credibility, he pulled back, he reconnoitered and planned his attack. And you didn't even see it coming. You have been made a fool."

She let the words wash over her, the old feelings threatening to resurrect. She wouldn't let them.

"This was not a war maneuver, Father. It was just a kiss. Just a simple kiss. And while it's embarrassing, you are blowing it all out of proportion."

"That's the kind of thinking that keeps you stuck where you are, Hope Highfield, living on a rundown piece of property with a driveway that is practically impassible, and having people pay you with eggs and loaves of bread instead of money."

"How people pay me is none of your business, Father. I have never asked you for a penny, and I never will."

He sighed. "I know, Hope. I just feel bad. I don't like to see someone take advantage of you. You go and stick your neck out, writing that silly letter to the paper, and then you let people walk all over you."

His words stung.

"It was not a silly letter. Someone is doing cruel and illegal things to animals, and I believe it has to stop."

"Well, I hope you get the result you desire, Hope. I hope it's worth it to you." His voice was soft for a moment, reminding her that beneath all the anger and despite their differences, they cared for each other.

"It's worth it, Dad." She rarely called him that.

"And if you have to be plastered all over the paper, could you try to look a little better? That hair, and no makeup! Your mother could have died."

"Sure, Dad," she mockingly agreed. "I'll make sure I have a facial and a new hairdo for the next reporter who comes sneaking around. It's the least I can do."

"Don't be flip, Hope Elizabeth. And come visit your mother soon. She misses you." He broke the connection.

Hope hung up the phone and ran her hands through her errant hair.

"You did okay," said Manny quietly, from a nearby desk. He was playing with a kitten, dangling a piece of string.

"He just doesn't understand. He's never understood."

Manny shrugged his shoulders. "People are different. They got good points and bad points. If you weren't just as stubborn as your old man, I might think you got switched by gypsies or something when you were born."

She smiled. "I'm sure there's a message in there somewhere for me, but right now I'm too tired to think about it. I need a nap before I'm ready to tackle the world again."

In the distance, she heard the sound of truck engines. "Is someone here?"

Manny stood. "Why don't you go take that nap. I'll go check, and take care of things here. Georgia and the pups are great, and everybody's fed and clean. Go get some rest."

She nodded and retreated to the house and her bedroom. Still dirty, and too tired to care about it, she curled up on the bed and was fast asleep by the time her head hit the pillow.

The persistent low rumbling sound penetrated her sleep and pulled her back from shadowy dreams. The sound of a train coming closer? Engine noises, followed by thumps and dragging sounds, brought her back to awareness after several hours of sleep.

Her mind fought to find reality, and she awoke. The engine sounds were still there. She stumbled to the door and looked out. She rubbed her eyes. What on God's green earth was going on?

There were a variety of trucks parked at Hope's Haven, there was dust in the air and the smell of diesel engines. A steam roller. Men with long rakes. In utter disbelief, she realized they were working on her driveway. They were almost finished working on her driveway. Fresh gray stone had been poured, raked, and rolled into her muddy rutted driveway, beginning at the entrance, and moving back past the clinic toward her house. They were busily finishing the last section.

The new gray pathway looked neat and even as far as the eye could see. And expensive. Hope felt a moment of panic.

She lunged out the door, still wearing her wrecked clothing from the calf delivery.

"Excuse me," she called excitedly but in vain to a tall man in a hardhat who was holding a clipboard. "Hey," she said angrily, finally getting his attention by plucking at his arm. "What exactly is going on here? I didn't contract for this work. There is no way—"

"No problem, lady," the man said easily, looking over at her disheveled attire. "We're just following orders. It's all taken care of. Ordered by Mr. Brandywine for the doctor."

"The doctor did not agree to this."

The man ran a tired hand over his sweating brow. "Look lady, we got an order, we do the work. That's how it works. You got a problem, take it up with the doctor. We're almost done here."

"I'm the doctor, Herbie," she said in a no-nonsense tone, reading the name embroidered on his shirt. "And I didn't order this driveway."

The man swallowed visibly. "Well, but, Mr. Brandy-wine . . ."

". . . Was overstepping his bounds, sir. And I'll take that up with Mr. Brandywine. Finish up and get this stuff out of here."

"Yes Ma'am." Herbie stammered, with a worried look on his face. "We thought we was doing the right thing."

It wasn't his fault. He had just been following orders.

"It's okay," she said softly. "I'll settle it with Mr. Brandy-wine."

Mr. Brandywine. Accustomed to giving orders, to being in charge, to being in control. Some people jumped for people like that. But not Hope Highfield. She had spent a lifetime earning her right to be in charge of her own life. Noah Brandywine didn't know who he was up against.

The machinery finally rumbled back out the new gray drive-way, leaving a trail of dust and grateful silence behind.

Hope went inside to shower and change her clothes, getting

ready to face Noah Brandywine when he arrived, as she was absolutely certain that he would.

Hope was right. It was only a short time later that she heard the purr of the Jaguar coming down the new gray driveway. She had taken a shower and changed her clothes, donning an embroidered peasant style blouse and a full navy blue skirt that ended below her knees. She slipped her feet into comfortable navy espadrilles, and glanced at the mirror as she passed. Her hair was brushed and shining, pulled casually back and tied at the nape of her neck with a bandana.

She wasn't really being vain, she told herself. It was more like a matter of pride, having been caught so many times looking her absolute worst in front of Mr. GQ, and in front of the entire readerships of the Ryerstown News, as a matter of fact.

She was going to face Noah Brandywine to straighten him out, and she had no intention of being caught at a disadvantage by looking like something the dog had dragged in, when he looked like a male fashion model.

Which at the very moment, he didn't. The car had stopped in front of the clinic, the door opened, and six feet-two inches of man climbed out. He was Noah's height, he was Noah's size. He was driving Noah's car. He even had Noah's face. But he sure didn't resemble the Noah that she had known!

This man, who looked like he was limping, was covered with smears of dirt. He was wearing muddy sneakers and a sweatshirt with a big ragged tear in the vicinity of the right rib cage.

She gasped in surprise.

He turned back to the car, bending over to retrieve something from the front seat. She got a glimpse of navy blue boxer shorts beneath the large tear in the back of his sweatpants.

What had happened? Torqued up as she was about the driveway, she couldn't help feeling sorry for the man who looked like he had fought with an alligator and lost. She stepped toward him.

He brought something out of the car. It was dark in color, and definitely—fuzzy. She shut her eyes and opened them again, focusing on the ball of fur that stood quietly by him. It was a dog. Big droopy eyes stared back at her from under the tuft of hair.

"You got a dog?" she asked in surprise.

"Maybe it's more like the dog got me." he sighed.

"You look awful. What happened to you?"

He waved his hand haphazardly in the air. "I went for a walk in the park."

"Were they detonating weapons in the park? Was there a riot?" She giggled.

He limped over to the steps by the clinic door, and suddenly turned and plopped down. The dog plopped beside him.

"This is what happens when people like me take walks in the park. People like me don't belong in the park. I was assaulted by a policeman. I was duped by a baby kitten. And I was adopted by this . . . dog."

"Does the dog have a name?" She bent down and scratched the scraggly head, and was rewarded by a look of adoration.

"I call him 'Hair.' I don't know why. It just came to me."

"Go figure." She sat down next to him on the step.

"Are you all right?" He really looked awful.

"All but my ego, I suppose. And a few bumps and bruises. I fell out of a tree. Never knew the ground could be so hard."

He looked at her then, noticing how fresh and pretty she looked, and enjoying the fresh clean scent of her as she sat beside him on the step.

"You look pretty."

"Thanks. I got tired of looking like a slob whenever you were around." He liked how she blushed.

"My turn, I suppose." He plucked at his torn sweatshirt. "Do you have any idea of how much money in clothes I've lost since I first set eyes on you?"

"I'm an undercover agent for Brooks Brothers. It's my solemn vow to increase sales."

It was amazing how easy it was to laugh with her. He told her, then, about the mission to the park, the fiascos, the tickets, and the dog.

"I'm sure he belongs to somebody." she said when he was

done. "Even though he's a mess at the moment, you can tell he's a nice dog and is used to a lot of love. Probably lost. I can put the word out, and odds are we'll find his owner."

"Or his hairdresser."

She laughed, petting the big dog. "Either one."

He was feeling better already. Despite dirt, grime, and the lasting effects of falling out of a tree, sitting here next to her and listening to her laugh was making him feel as if all was well in the world.

He looked out at the driveway that sprawled before him, looking neat and smooth and more like an airport runway than a guerilla warfare minefield. He may not have been able to bond with this animal thing, but he could effect change. He had fixed the driveway.

Feeling just the slightest bit pleased with himself, he said, "Driveway looks great, doesn't it?"

Armageddon. Mount Vesuvius. Sonic boom. In a flash, the peace in the air exploded, and Hope erupted.

"And where on earth do you get off thinking you can insert yourself into my life and make decisions for me? Who asked you to fix the driveway? Did it ever occur to you that I did not want the driveway fixed? Did it ever occur to you that it wasn't your business? Did it ever occur to you that there was absolutely nothing wrong with the driveway, and that it didn't need to be fixed?" Finished with her tirade, mostly because she was ready to hyperventilate, she took a breath.

"Are you done?" the muddy man said quietly. "May I respond to your points with two 'I don't knows' and three 'no's.' Especially to the last point. It didn't need to be fixed? Are you out of your mind?"

"If I'm out of my mind, then that's my right, too. I am an adult. I am independent. I can make my own decisions, and I don't need anybody second guessing me or telling me what's best for me. I fought those battles all my life, and you, Noah Brandywine, are not going to interfere with the way I live."

"Point well taken. I sense some baggage here. I didn't mean to overstep my bounds. I apologize on all points aforementioned. Except the last one."

She looked like she was going to growl at him.

"Lighten up, Hope Highfield. You have every right to have your driveway look like a pint-sized Grand Canyon if you choose, but you can't deny that it was a mess. And if I've offended your sensibilities so much by forcing a gift on you, you can pay me for it."

She frowned, sticking her lip out. "I don't have the money."

"So I gathered from that Manny kid. Don't you charge for your services? What kind of a business are you running here?"

"People pay with what they can pay. I've got a year's supply of eggs, the clinic gets painted once a year, and I've got coupons for free tattoos for the rest of my natural life, in case I ever get into body art. I'm not in this for the money. I'm in it because I want to make an impact. I want to help living creatures that need help. It's a higher-level actualization thing. A crass materialist such as yourself probably can't identify with this sort of thing."

"The air is heavy with sarcasm, Dr. Doolittle. Even crass corporate types such as myself contribute to the world's causes, you know. I'm a big supporter of the United Way."

"I believe I saw your picture in the paper last year, publicly giving your donation. Nice press. And the woman on your arm was wearing enough jewelry to feed a third-world country for a year."

"The women on my arm at any time can wear or not wear anything that they like. Nice shot of us in today's news, didn't you think?"

He had been wanting to bring up the issue of the picture of the stolen kiss, and she had given him an opening.

She was blushing to the roots of her hair. He suddenly found himself imagining kissing that flushed pink neck, nibbling on that adorable ear.

"That was so embarrassing," she said softly, and it came out almost like a whisper.

"Not the kiss, I hope," he said, looking into her eyes. "Just the reporter."

She couldn't even speak. She licked her lips slightly, not

knowing that the action practically drove him out of his mind. His pulse was pounding as if he were a randy teenager.

He had come to apologize, to make things better, not to make things more complicated. He knew better. He should have better judgement. They were diametrically opposed in just about every way that mattered. Just about.

But he couldn't help himself. Like a magnet in an uncontrollable force field, he leaned toward her, capturing her lips in a kiss.

It was as if her body didn't need breath anymore. Her bones turned to butter. She melted against him, turning toward him where they sat on the steps to meet his embrace, her mouth welcoming his kiss. Her arms went around his neck, holding on for dear life, her fingers curling in his wavy dark hair.

She tingled from the top of her head to the tip of her toes. If she hadn't been sitting, she would have collapsed on the ground.

This is a bad idea, her brain hollered. *I've got to get hold of myself.*

But all she really wanted to get hold of was the six foot-two inch hunk of man who was awakening yearnings that she had only ever imagined. His arms were possessively around her, his big hands stroking her back, her shoulders, her arms.

"Ah, Hope," he murmured, with his lips lightly touching hers, "You feel so good."

It was the insanity of it all that finally brought her to a stop. With difficulty, she placed her hands on his broad chest, and pushed to put some space between them, bringing her head back and stopping his kiss. Immediately she felt the loss.

Was she crazy? Only yesterday her picture had been taken and splashed over today's newspapers. And now this. An even more compromising shot would be a great candidate for the tabloid spreads at the grocery store.

And that was only the publicity angle. What about her own ethics? Her own values? Her ability to control her own destiny? This man stood for everything she had fought hard to escape. She didn't even like him; and yet here she was kissing him and wanting even more. What was wrong with her?

He hadn't said a word since the kiss had ended, just sitting next to her, and staring at her with eyes full of questions.

Such intense eyes. So what was so objectionable about him? He was afraid of animals, yet he had helped her with Georgia's puppy delivery. He admitted he had gone to the park to get used to people and their pets. Wasn't that a sign he wasn't a total loss in the animal department?

He had bulldozed (literally) the repairs of her driveway in that bossy way of his, yet he had apologized when she had freaked out about it. Did that mean he wasn't hopelessly controlling?

And he had absolutely denied having anything to do with the unethical animal testing. Could she trust him? She hadn't found the evidence to acquit him, but she hadn't found the evidence to convict him, either.

Would he dare to keep in touch with her like this, to kiss her until she was practically melted into a puddle on her own clinic steps, if he had a guilty conscience? Or was he just keeping an eye on her, making sure he knew in advance of any further steps she might take that would discredit his beloved company?

She was confused, and she didn't like the feeling.

An ounce of prevention is worth a pound of cure, she thought to herself. This kissing has got to stop. She looked into the deep dark eyes that were still staring at her, as if waiting for her to make a response.

Her nerve endings tingled. She'd be best to simply stay away from this man who had such a magnetic pull on her, making her do and think things that were totally out of character.

Vaguely, she looked around, noting that Hair the Dog, Billie the Goat, and three striped cats had banded together in front of them, watching them with interest.

"Glad we're able to entertain you guys," she said to the animal audience through her teeth.

"We should sell tickets." Noah Brandywine finally spoke.

She turned and looked at him then, trying to find the words

that would break the spell, and keep her from doing anything more ridiculous than she already had.

"Would you like to go out to dinner?" her voice said.

Had her mind been taken over by aliens?

"Great idea. But do we have to take the peanut gallery?" he asked, his head motioning to the clump of animals that stood by them in the grass.

She laughed. "No, their table manners are even worse than mine. We'll leave them here. Manny is coming to do chores soon."

He stood, groaning as he unfolded his body. "I'm not going to make it a habit to fall out of trees. Give me an hour to go home and get cleaned up, and we'll go somewhere nice."

Her heart was hammering. One side of her brain was dying to take back her words and send him away. The other side was leaping with excitement at the prospect of spending time with him. She stalled.

"I have to walk to the back of the property and check on a nest of baby ducks. I want to be sure the sound of the heavy machinery didn't disturb them too much. Want to come?"

She could tell by the look on his face that he had had just about enough of animals for the day. But the look vanished, he squared his shoulders and held his head high. He looked like a knight getting ready for battle.

"All right," he said bravely. "Introduce me to the fowl."

She kept a straight face, but inwardly, her heart smiled. She led him up the winding path that was located behind the office, traveling slightly uphill, past blossoming bushes that smelled of honeysuckle, over roots of massive trees that sprawled overhead like a leafy green awning. Little specks of late afternoon sunshine occasionally peeked through, casting scattered sunrays over the path.

Noah walked behind her, watching the gentle sway of her hips as she moved easily up the path, watching the straight spine, the feminine curve of her neck. All around him was quiet. The peaceful, soul-soothing sound of silence was punctuated only by occasional chirps of a curious bird. He liked it.

He surprised himself with the thought. For this, he would face hairy dogs with slobbery tongues. For this, he would face climbing kittens. Maybe not the goat. He'd draw the line at the goat. But for this, he would face ducks.

The path started down a slope, and after a few minutes, he could hear the familiar rush of the river somewhere before them. He knew that sound—from his house, as well as from the plant—the river sound. He caught up to Hope as they rounded the last bend, his long strides bringing him right behind her. He was close enough to get a whiff of the clean-smelling scent of her, and he had to fight the urge to put his hands on her shoulders to pull her back toward him so that he could nuzzle his head in her hair.

But it wasn't time for that. It was time for . . . ducks.

And suddenly, there they were. Ducks everywhere. They reached the riverbank, which was steep and filled with bushes this far up the river. Nestled in the undergrowth, the ducks had nested. He had expected to see little fluffy, helpless things, sitting placidly in their nest, beaks open expectantly for the mama ducks to feed them. But these were *not* fluffy things. These were just little ducks. Smaller, darker—but not placid. As soon as they caught site of the visitors, they jumped into rank behind the mother duck with a whirlwind of commotion.

Squawk! Squawk! Squeak!

All the lithe little bodies zipped around, ending up in an arc-shaped line behind mama. And she was heading their way.

"Hi, Dolores!" called Hope softly. "All the babies look good. One, two . . ." she counted, up to "eight, nine, ten."

Noah felt the perspiration begin to gather on his forehead.

"Squawk! Squawk!" Ten little bodies (and one rather large one) had moved methodically up the path, and were now surrounding them, like warriors at a massacre.

Hope squatted comfortably and put out her fingertips for the revolving ducks to investigate. Noah swallowed hard.

Had she not ever seen Alfred Hitchcock's movie "The Birds?"

"Aren't they adorable? I helped Dolores a few years ago when she had a broken wing, and we were very careful to keep her able to take care of herself in the wild. She fends well for herself, but she is still tame in some respects. Although when the babies were first born, I kept my distance. Baby ducks bond to the first moving thing they see. I made sure that was Dolores!"

He had a vision then, of Hope moving around with a string of ducks following her everywhere she went. And why not? Was she not the Pied Piper of the animal kingdom?

He realized, suddenly, that he felt all right. He didn't pet them, but then, he didn't mind them either.

They weren't so bad, these ducks. They just seemed to waddle and quack and squawk, and then go their way. He watched the little line retreat, their little back ends rocking back and forth as they followed their mother back past their nest and down the river bank.

Plop! Plop! Plop! One after another they hit the current, looking like a little miniature (and feathered) armada.

Hope stood and turned toward him.

"They're fine. In fact, they're great."

She looked up into his face then, knowing full well the effort it had taken him to experience the flock. She raised her hand and gently stroked his cheek.

"You're fine too, Noah Brandywine. In fact, you also are great. Thank you for meeting my ducks."

He covered her hand with his own, and then slowly pulled it toward his lips. Gently, with a touch as soft as a feather, he kissed her palm.

She sighed.

They headed back down the path together, and he kept her hand in his. It felt like it belonged there. For this, he would meet the ducks any old day. In fact, he might even decide he liked ducks.

They arrived back at the clinic, and Hope looked at her watch.

"I'll be back in an hour. And we'll go somewhere nice."

"OK. Since I'm wearing a skirt for once, I'd hate to have it go to waste!" Her light tone didn't match the storm in her stomach.

"Absolutely. I'll be right back."

He walked to the car then, saying over his shoulder. "I don't know what's going on here, Hope Highfield, but you've cast a spell on me. Not into witchcraft, are you?"

"Not yet, but you never know."

The Jag roared to life, and he sped down the newly smooth drive, his mind in overdrive. The kiss had knocked him out, and he had wanted to keep kissing her, right there, right out in the open, right in front of the animals, the neighbors, even the AP news. He was going to have to get a hold of himself if he was going to deal with this totally aggravating and totally unnerving woman who could tie him up in knots like nothing he had ever known before.

He thought of her as he had last seen her, standing there in that flowing skirt, her slim brown calves exposed.

No, Hope Highfield, the skirt did not go to waste.

All he could think about all the way home was the amazing Hope Highfield. He'd be lucky if he could keep the Jag on the road with the thoughts blasting through his head, and even luckier still if he could make it through dinner without embarrassing himself.

And the funny thing was, he was looking forward to the challenge. And he was *not* going to order duck.

Noah pulled the car into the garage at his house. When he got out of the car, he looked down at his destroyed sweat suit and muddy grass-stained sneakers.

With a shrug, he stripped them off and plopped them into the trash can that stood in the garage. Throwaway clothes, that's what he needed for visiting Hope's Haven.

Barefooted, and clad only in his boxer shorts and undershirt, he climbed the short flight of steps that led into the kitchen of his house.

Mentally he was planning the outfit he would wear to dine with Hope; his grey slacks in the lightweight wool, the imported Italian shoes he had picked up on his last trip to Rome, and the handmade silk shirt that was a soft shade of gray to go with the slacks. He wanted to look his best. Classy, but casual. He thought of Hope in her charming peasant blouse and his mouth began to water. He was turning into quite a lecher in his old age. He began to whistle.

Stepping across the cool tile floor of the kitchen, several things registered in his wandering mind.

Soft music was playing from somewhere within, and he knew for certain that he had not left the sound system activated. The unmistakable scent of Brandywine perfume was drifting in the air. He looked across the kitchen toward the open door of the living room. Draped on the back of one of the chairs, he could see a silk scarf. Expensive silk. Feminine.

Uh oh, he thought.

He stepped through the door, his worst suspicions confirmed. Cheryl sat draped in one of his designer leather chairs.

"You're finally back," she said in a bored tone. She looked up and noticed his attire—or lack of it.

"And almost naked, I see." She smiled, but the look didn't reach her eyes. "You're taking me to dinner, darling, in case you've forgotten. To make up for your ill-advised smooch with the trollop vet in the paper. And you may as well get dressed. No hanky panky with this lady until you've made good."

"Cheryl." He stood speechless in his underwear, wanting to interrupt the flow of words, but at a loss as to what to say. His mind was as garbled as yesterday's spaghetti as he looked at her. She was beautiful. Totally in control. And controlling. Every hair was in place. He wished she were anywhere but here.

He thought of dark hair suddenly, escaping wildly in tendrils. He thought of oversized boots, and a pair of slim tanned legs beneath a peasant skirt.

"Cheryl," he began again. "I didn't expect you at this time. In fact, I have to admit I had forgotten we had considered dinner tonight."

Her catlike eyes narrowed.

"You forgot me?"

"It's been a busy day. And it's not done. I just came home

to change, and I've got to go back. You know how I am about business."

He was usually so in control, but he didn't feel like it at the moment. He didn't like standing here in his underwear, babbling.

"Business?" she said coyly. "I called the office several times this afternoon. Seems they didn't know where you were. Actually, Frank was the one who came by and let me in. He obviously felt badly that you hadn't been in touch."

Frank had let her in? He made a mental note to talk to his security chief in the morning.

"Couldn't be helped." His anger was mounting, and the feeling gave him back some of his control. "I was in the field." While this was literally true, he had no intention of elaborating on it. "Is your car here?"

"I parked it on the street," she said calmly, but her eyes were flashing. "Are you trying to say that you are standing me up for dinner, Noah Brandywine?"

She stood now, and crossed the room to him, draping her arms seductively around his neck, her fingers making little circles on his exposed skin.

"Well, perhaps," she went on in a low voice, "You have time for a little before you get back out into the field."

Slowly, he raised his arms to hers, and brought her arms down.

"This is not a good time, Cheryl," he said quietly, but firmly. "Maybe a raincheck."

Her temper snapped. "A raincheck? I don't think so. You're a creep, Noah Brandywine."

He picked up her coat and scarf. "Let me help you with your coat."

She knew by the timbre of his voice that she had gone too far. Something had changed in Noah, but she didn't know what. And right now, she didn't care. Her anger fueled her toward the door.

"A raincheck?" she screeched. "It'll be a cold day in hell before I accept that, Noah Brandywine. You're going to be sorry for this."

Then she was gone.

He breathed a sigh of relief. He hadn't handled it well, he knew, but at least it was over. And it would take a hurricane, a tornado, a tsunami, and a cold day in hell before he would call her again, raincheck or not.

He turned off the sound system, opened a window to get rid of the scent of her cologne, and rushed to the bathroom to get ready for his dinner date with Hope Highfield.

When Noah left Hope's Haven, Hope had turned her attention to checking on her animals. Her heart warmed, as it always did, as she scurried around feeding her charges and doling out love in large amounts. There were no animals in crisis, as there had been no major surgeries on the weekend and no additional animals rescued from the river.

Manny arrived on his dilapidated bike.

"Yo, Doc!" he hollered from the newly smooth driveway. "You win the lottery or something? How'd you manage this, anyway?"

Hope heard the bike crash to the ground, a familiar sound.

"Stop it, Billie. Leave me alone. You gotta teach this goat some manners one of these days."

She looked up and smiled at him as he came in the door. He stopped suddenly and stared at her.

"Uh oh."

"What's wrong?"

"I was about to ask you the same thing, Doc. You're wearing a dress. Did somebody die?"

"I wear dresses occasionally, Manuel Perez. Don't make such a big deal."

"Yeah, right. And the Pope has waterskis."

"Maybe he does. How would you know?"

Manny ignored her flipness.

"And the driveway. You wanna explain that? You could run the Indy Five Hundred on that thing. We gonna sell tickets?"

"Again, no big deal. Noah Brandywine did it. I was ticked

off at first. He didn't even ask. But he seemed to think we needed it."

"At least the man's not blind. And do you know how much an alignment on one of those fancy imported cars is going for these days? Darn right we needed it. Either that or build a bridge. So how are we gonna pay for it?"

"He wanted to do it for nothing. But I said I'd figure out a way to pay him. I'm still working on that."

"He wouldn't be interested in a few tattoos, would he?"

He saw her wind up to throw the brush she had been using to groom a collie. "Naw, I guess not," he said.

"We're going out to dinner. At a restaurant. He went home to dress."

"Uh oh."

"Stop saying that. What do you mean, uh oh?"

"Look. I work for a perfectly nice, if a little eccentric, vet who does the same thing day after day after day. Then all of a sudden, she's causing corporate uprisings, giving out hot kisses that end up on the front page of the newspaper, playing double-o-seven at local companies at night, repaving driveways with no money in the bank, and going out to dinner at a restaurant, and all on account of that dapper-dressing rich guy who you say that you can't stand. In Brooklyn, where I come from, we kinda think of these things as signs to pay attention to. You're acting like more of a nut case than usual. Who wouldn't say "uh oh" to that?"

Hope nodded thoughtfully. "I suppose it does look strange."

"Stranger than fiction. I hope you know what you are getting into, Doc. I don't know if I trust this guy. Just because he's a good kisser."

The brush flew, hitting Manny in the shoulder.

"So maybe he's not a good kisser," he laughed. "Oh, no," he yelped playfully as he saw her lift up a water bucket with every intention of heaving it. "I apologize. It's all normal. Absolutely normal. Put the bucket down, Hope."

She obeyed. Together they cornered Billie and got her corralled. She introduced Manny to Hair, who proceeded to roll over and shake hands and do tricks at the thought of getting dinner. Tomorrow, she promised herself, she would attempt to find his owner.

They visited Georgia, checked over the pups, who were all thriving, and rotated the hungry babies so they were sure that each had had a chance to feed. Even the smallest one was healthy and active.

Back in the office, she called Georgia's owner in the hospital and gave him a report on his Great Dane and her brood. The elderly man, whose surgery had gone well, chuckled at the news.

When her chores were done, she took a minute and rebrushed her hair, putting on a light dose of lipstick, the only concession to makeup that she ever made.

Manny whistled when she came back into the office. "Uh oh."

"There you go again. This is just a nice normal dinner, that's all."

The sound of the Jag coming up the drive reached their ears. She grabbed her shawl and purse and said goodbye to Manny, bounding down the steps.

"And I'm just a nice, normal teenager," said the boy under his breath as he watched her go. "Be careful, Doc. Be careful."

But she didn't hear his words, because she had climbed into the waiting Jag and was already rolling down the long, freshly paved, but unpaid, driveway.

She noticed that the car smelled of leather and the intoxicating smell of Noah's aftershave as soon as she got in. She was glad to see him, her pulse quickening, and her tongue momentarily tied. Was this for real? Hope Highfield had never been so taken with a man.

"You look wonderful," Noah said quietly, and she met his eyes with a smile.

"Manny thinks I'm nuts, consorting with the enemy."

"I'm not the enemy, Hope." He reached over and squeezed her hand. "I made a reservation at a nice little place upriver a ways. It'll take us a while to get there, but I think you'll find it worth the trip. It's built into the riverbank, and there is a wonderful waterfall."

"Hmm," she said in response. "Sounds nice."

The car stereo was playing a soft tune, and she put her head back on the headrest and relaxed, enjoying the scenery, the music, and most of all, the man next to her.

It wasn't that she had no experience with men. She had had boyfriends in her college days, had even thought she had been in love at one point. But the relationship had soured in the end. She had had strong motivations to succeed, to build her career, to follow her dedication to saving animals. Her father had never understood, and as it had turned out, her so-called boyfriend hadn't either. He'd wanted his needs, his career to come first, and had constantly criticized and disapproved of her decisions and her responsibilities. Finally, she had said goodbye to him with a hardened heart and the feeling that a man's unwavering need was to control. And she wouldn't be controlled.

So she had decided that relationships weren't all they were cracked up to be, and that sex simply wasn't that important either.

But since her blood still returned to the boiling point at even the memory of Noah's kiss, she was rapidly rethinking her hypothesis. A man who could turn her body to playdough with a kiss might be worth trying to get to know.

She nestled down in the well-padded seat and watched the scenery fly by, the incomparable summer beauty of early evening, when the sun began to dip, throwing its last rays with high delight, making greens greener and blues deeper. Tonight, she had every intention of enjoying herself, despite Manny's dire warnings.

They rode quietly for several more minutes, until Noah broke the silence. "Do you like seafood?"

"Love it. How about you?"

"Sure. Although I never had it until I was an adult. We had simple fare as a kid. Not a well stocked larder."

"So you've implied. Any brothers or sisters?"

"Just me and my mom. That was hard enough. My mom literally worked herself to death trying to raise me. She died when I was ten. I was in foster homes then for a while."

"That must have been hard."

"I suppose. Funny thing is, I don't even remember much of it. I just put my nose to the grindstone and decided that I was going to be a success. Get rich. And I did."

"Was getting rich your only goal?" She looked at his profile in the close duskiness of the car. The sun was going down and nighttime was approaching.

He looked surprised at her question. "Of course. Money means power. Money means success. Don't tell me you don't understand that concept. You are Hugh Highfield's daughter. His name is practically synonymous with money."

She looked at him sadly. Would he ever understand? With a childhood deprived of necessities, money and power must have looked so good. But it wasn't always.

"Money isn't the goal for some people, Noah. I grew up in a big house with everything that money could buy. But I hated it. I didn't want the life that was mapped out for me by my parents. I didn't want coming out parties, and the exclusive life of snotty country clubs and society friends. I wanted to choose my own path in life."

"Sure, it's easy to say that when you're born with a silver spoon in your mouth, when you have family to back you up."

She shook her head, not willing to explain further. She could not put into words the painful years she had suffered, the fights, the anguish over not being able to make her own choices in the framework of her father's rules. She had had to leave it all, eventually, and had never regretted it. But the memory of the painful process was wrenching to her soul.

She looked out the window and commented on the scenery instead, effectively changing the subject.

They were traveling north, on Hope's side of the river, where the road was windy and scenic in the last rays of light. There were few houses here where trees overtook the sloping banks of the river, some that had stood for hundreds of years. Through the undergrowth, the rushing water could be glimpsed occasionally.

A few more miles up the river, they passed the National Pharmaceuticals Company, a low, rambling structure of red brick that sat near the road, its back facing the river at a break in the trees. There were two trucks parked in its vacant lot, and no sign of activity around it.

It was another company on Hope's list of places to investigate that was in close enough proximity to be involved with the animals that had come ashore at Hope's Haven.

Noah noticed her scrutiny of the place.

"They make bandages, Hope. Not likely that they would do experimenting on animals."

"Well, someone is. So it has to be investigated."

"You mean I'm not the only person you've planned on torturing with your accusations?"

She had to admit she felt a little guilty about her shoot from the hip media charges at Brandywine Beauty. She knew Noah had taken a beating financially with the bad press, and he'd already admitted how important money was to him. And it didn't seem likely, getting to know him, that he'd have anything to do with such a plan.

"I've learned my lesson, and won't attack without evidence again," she said contritely. "There was nothing to tie your company to the abuse except for my imagination, I suppose. And I was so insulted at being ignored by your office. But that didn't make you guilty."

An apology from the strong-minded vet? He realized what her words had cost her.

"Thanks. Apology accepted."

"Of course, the questions still haven't been answered. And I intend to find those answers."

"I should have guessed." He smiled, keeping his eyes straight ahead on the windy road.

"Could I convince you to join detective forces with me?"

He sighed. "Hope, I'm not a detective. I'm a businessman. I make money. I don't detect."

"Okay." She'd do it herself. She was used to that. But it was a shame, she thought, looking over at him again. He would have looked cute in a "Magnum PI" baseball cap!

In a few minutes, they reached the restaurant. Turning left, away from the river, and up a long, winding drive, Hope got her first glimpse of Skye House, which sat high above the river valley. Cheerful lights beckoned them from the windows. They parked the car and went inside, where they were led to a table that overlooked the river valley. Darkness had set in, the scene sparkled with the sprinkling of lights that glowed from scattered houses down below. It was beautiful.

The restaurant had a Scottish motif, with plaids on the table-tops and the heavy coats of arms from several clans hanging on the high stone walls. There was a fire in the giant fireplace that cast a rosy glow as well as a little welcomed heat. The air had chilled as the sun went down.

The restaurant wasn't crowded. They dined in the light of a small oil lamp on their table, enjoying their meal and talking about mundane, first date things. They discussed movies, and weather, and local spots in town, and stayed away from any emotional or opinion-charged topics.

The time flew by. As they left, with the hearty best wishes from the friendly host and staff echoing in their ears, it was almost hard to leave the quiet and relaxing place.

The ride back to Hope's Haven was quiet and peaceful.

"That was nice," he said simply as they neared her drive. "I had a good time with you, Hope."

She blushed in the darkness of the car. "Me too. And we didn't even fight. Not once."

He grinned. "Not once. Think we could dare to try it again?"

"Maybe. Let's see how things go."

The truth was, there was nothing she would rather do than spend more time with Noah Brandywine. And she didn't trust that feeling—not at all.

He stopped the Jaguar in front of her door.

"Should I come in?"

Panic welled inside of her. Her senses flared. The thought of being alone with him, the kisses, her lack of control. . . . Her emotions were a mess, and she was wise enough to know it.

"Bad idea, Noah. I don't know where we're going with this thing. And I'm not a casual type of woman."

"I know."

"But I'm not a prude either."

"I know that too."

She blushed again, thankful that he couldn't see it.

"Maybe next time." Her heart quickened as she said the words.

"I'll look forward to it," he said softly.

She turned toward him in the car, and she could tell he was going to kiss her again. But she couldn't let him. She'd be lost, falling down the rabbit hole at the very least. He had that sort of effect on her. She had to figure it out first, before she dared to risk her reaction to his touch. Because once he started touching her, she had a very strong feeling that she'd never want him to stop!

She opened the car door and got out before he knew it. She didn't even want him to walk her to the door. She didn't trust her own resolve.

"Bye, Noah. Thanks for dinner and a great evening," she said in the window of the car.

"Don't run away, Hope."

"I'm not running. This isn't running. In some circles they call me the Highfield Flash."

"I can imagine." He smiled. "I'll be back, Hope."

"I'll be here."

The Jag roared to life, and he pulled out, watching her step into the clinic to check on her charges before ending her night.

"I'll be back, Hope Highfield, and no matter how much you doubt me, or how fast you run, I'll catch you," he said under his breath.

When Hope walked in the clinic door, her heart singing with possibilities, she wasn't ready for what she found.

Manny sat on the floor of the clinic, a plugged-in portable heater throwing gusts of heat through her office. He was soaking wet, and his teeth were chattering. There were blankets bunched up around him, and engulfed in the many folds, as well as filling his lap, were dozens of baby animals, squealing with discomfort and gasping for air. One after another, he was lifting them, dabbing each back with a swab of antiseptic. He saw her and his eyes filled with relief.

"It's bad, Doc," he said through shivering lips. "I saved as many as I could. You could hear them in the river. Dozens and dozens. And all with these terrible sores on their backs. Whatever this batch was tested with, it was bad stuff. They've blistered something awful. I've gotten them clean and warm, and now I'm trying to medicate them, take care of the pain."

She didn't say a word, not trusting her voice. She stepped quickly to her drug cabinet and pulled out a box of syringes and medicine, thankful that she had come right home. Manny could provide first aid, but some of these poor creatures were in need of more sophisticated medical care.

Within seconds she was administering doses of medicine, counteracting the allergic reaction, and lessening the pain. As she and Manny worked together, one animal after another was treated. They slowly calmed and huddled together in the blanket-filled boxes they prepared. Never in her life had she seen such needless pain and destruction. How many others had perished in the river, after having to endure such pain? The thought made her sick.

"We are going to get to the bottom of this, Manny," she said with determination. "This cannot go on. No matter what the cost, the person responsible will be found and stopped."

Manny nodded silently, his face tense and tight.

He looked at her seriously, his wet clothes no longer dripping but still hanging wetly from his body.

He had seen the way her eyes were glowing when she first came in the door. She wasn't going to like what he had to tell her.

"I hope you mean that, Doc. Because I have a strong feeling that there will be a cost."

"What do you mean, you hope I mean it? Of course I mean it. Why would you say a thing like that?"

Taking a deep breath, he reached in the pocket of his soggy jeans.

"Because these were floating in the river, too."

With sad eyes, he held out his hand, holding several plastic bags, each about eight inches square, and all bearing the distinctive logo of Brandywine Beauty Products.

Chapter Six

Hope's hands felt cold. Her chest felt tight. An icy blanket of betrayal fell over her. Noah Brandywine was tricking her. He had slithered into her life and into her heart like the snake that he was. He had gotten close to her, broken down her defenses, put her off guard. She had actually begun to believe in him. And he was guilty.

She took in a slow, deep breath, knowing that Manny was watching her, knowing that there was much to be done. Hope Highfield, the doctor of veterinary medicine, took over, her feelings cast aside.

"Get a new box of syringes from the cabinet behind my desk," she said quickly. She opened the nearby refrigerator with one arm, grabbing a vial from the shelf on the door.

Manny was already across the room. She squatted down

beside the small wet victims, speaking gently to them. "It'll be all right, little guys. It'll be all right."

Manny began handing her syringes rhymically, and she filled each one and gently gave the kittens a dose, one after another. They worked together silently, the only noise in the room the occasional gentle words to a frantic victim.

"Is the incubator warmed? These guys are really chilled."

"It's ready," said Manny, as he began lifting the medicated kittens to the large incubator by the back door. Soon the group of rescuees were snuggled together peacefully in the artificial warmth, their pain momentarily eased, their panic calmed. Healing had begun.

"We'll know by morning," Hope said, "how many will make it. Thank goodness you were here, Manny. Thank goodness you found them."

And the plastic bags, she thought to herself, feeling a momentary pang in the vicinity of her broken heart.

She'd contact the police in the morning, as well as the SPCA and other animal support agencies. In her opinion, it was unethical to do scientific testing on animals in any circumstances, but there were studies that were not illegal. They were governed, however, by strict guidelines about what was humane and how those studies were to be carried out. And the torture and subsequent disposal of the subjects that had been rescued tonight broke every one of those guidelines.

She would make Noah Brandywine pay. And she would make sure that he would never take part in such a study again.

"I'm going to stay here and watch them, Doc," Manny announced when things were quiet.

She nodded. She told him she'd call his foster parents and let them know. It wouldn't be the first time. Manny had a cot in the storeroom behind the office that he had used on many an occasion, beginning on the first day that he had popped into her life almost five years before.

She'd chased him with a hammer in her hands, on that first auspicious occasion, having come upon him committing vandalism with a spray can on the back of her clinic wall.

She'd been a brand new vet, and had just taken over the

property that was now Hope's Haven. She'd been valiantly wrestling with a large roll of fence wire while attempting to attach it to the old wooden rail fence that surrounded the property, to protect her small animals from the cars whizzing by on the road.

Manny had been a thirteen-year-old runaway, aggressive, hostile, and desperate. A street orphan who had gotten himself on the wrong side of a Brooklyn gang, he'd run away and had gotten off the bus at Ryerstown when his money ran out.

New town, old tricks. Hope had caught him with the spray paint, taking out his anger about a life he saw as hopeless on the environment.

"I didn't hire a painter," she had told him sarcastically, facing down the tough-looking youth.

"And if I did, I wouldn't have him painting with those colors, that's for sure."

"What's it to you, lady? I ain't bothering nobody. Take off."

"You're bothering me. This is my place. That's my wall. And that's your paint, see?"

Even at thirteen he had loomed over her, but she hadn't cowered or backed down when he approached her, anger in his eyes.

She faced him, eyes locked. She saw a pathetic, confused young boy, the bleakness in his eyes warring with his need to act out. Was he dangerous? Most probably. Like an injured animal, a fox caught in a trap, striking out at the closest target was an instinct. But she had removed many a fox from a trap, and she hadn't gotten bitten yet. You just had to know how to approach a creature in pain.

His clothes were old, his thin frame gave him a gaunt look. When was the last time this growing boy had had a good meal?

There you go, Hope Elizabeth, her father's voice echoed in her brain. *Trying to save the world. Trying to do the impossible. Send him on his way. Don't get involved.*

"You don't happen to know how to do normal painting, by any chance, do you?" she asked in a pained voice. "Or better yet, do you know how to hammer? Because my arms are killing me and I've still got a lot to do."

He'd stared at her blankly.

"I mean, if you're not too busy, it could really be a help. I would pay you, and maybe get us some sandwiches. I don't know about you, but I'm hungry."

She could see him, swallow. He *was* hungry. But he still didn't speak.

A cat had poked its head through the underbrush and approached him to investigate.

"That's Lulu. She was here when I moved in. Thinks she owns the place. I don't know how she's going to react to the rest in the long run. There's five more I rescued from the pound as of today. But I've got to get this fence done, so they don't get hit by a car."

"What kind of place is this?' he said, a soft Spanish accent to his voice.

"It's Hope's Haven. I'm a vet. It's a place for animals to get well, or to be safe until I can find them a home."

He nodded, as if he were thinking. Then he turned to walk away, back toward the river, spray can in hand.

"Well, I'm going to go eat," she chattered on to his back. She put the hammer down by the fence rail where she had stopped working, and looked over toward the wall he had painted with wild swirls of army green. "No, I really don't like that ugly color. When I paint that wall, it'll be beige, nice and light and clean looking."

He was gone. She went back to the house. The truth was, she *was* hungry, and her arm was aching from hammering. She needed a break. She made herself a sandwich and gulped it down. Then she made another one, stuffing it full of extra meat and cheese. She wrapped it and placed it in a paper bag, adding a bag of chips and a cold soda.

She sprinted back to the fence, and placed the bag next to the fence rail, and then returned to the clinic office to do another item on her mile-long "to do" list.

Less than an hour later, she smiled when she heard the

steady sound of hammering in the distance. It wasn't the first time she'd used food as bait!

She walked back to the fence at dinnertime. The hammering had stopped. She found the areas deserted, and the fence wire totally installed. The lunch bag, of course, was gone.

Laughing, she placed another bagged meal at the fence post with the word *THANKS* printed on its side. Then she tacked a ten dollar bill to the wooden post near the bag.

When she checked the next day, the food and money were gone, and the back wall of the clinic boasted a fresh, even coat of beige paint. It looked great. She left one last note, "Come see me if you want more work," tacking it to the wall with a twenty dollar bill.

It took three days for him to appear at the clinic door.

It took three months to convince him that he could trust Hope's judgment, and to agree to move into the foster home she had located for him. With the determination of a pitbull, she had tackled the county children's services to help him to get settled. He had left no family behind in Brooklyn, and was totally alone in the world.

He had worked part time for Hope ever since, being enrolled in school for the first time, and finally having the stability of family life that had escaped him before.

Manny was an amazing young man. He was also an angry one. And right now, Noah Brandywine was the object of that fury. She watched the determined young man bed down for the night, and knew there was nothing she could say to change his mind.

He had rescued the injured animals, and he was going to stand watch over them in case they needed him during the night. Case closed.

She gave him a high five sign.

"Good night, Manny. You'll call me if you need me?"

"You can count on it, Doc. See you in the morning."

With the crisis over, she crossed the new gray driveway and headed for the quiet of her apartment, knowing she would have to face the pain in her heart.

*   *   *

"I saw you in the paper the other day," said Hope's friend Meridith on the phone early Monday morning. "Lovely man you were kissing," she crooned. "Aren't you going to share with your best friend?"

Meridith was a prominent attorney with a corner office in a prestigious law firm located on the sixteenth floor of a Philadelphia highrise.

"Share? You can have him," Hope said contemptfully.

Meridith's smooth voice laughed at her.

These days they had different lifestyles and moved in different circles. But in childhood they had been inseparable. They had shared everything, thoughts and dreams, clothes and classroom notes. Even boys.

"Remember Henry the Fourth in seventh grade? We shared him, remember?" Meridith teased.

And so they had. Their formal dancing class had been short of boys. Henry the Fourth (known in *Who's Who* circles as Henry Ballentine Fulbraith IV, heir to a banking fortune) had been a good-natured, chubby boy, his face mottled with stubborn acne despite the attention of the best dermatologists money could buy. He had always been the last chosen as a partner by the "debutante dollies" of Miss Panarelli's School of Classic Dance.

Hope and Meridith had both abhorred the parent-dictated dancing class, for different reasons. Hope had hated the formality, the white gloves, the strict adherence to social propriety and haughty behavior.

"It's exactly what you need, Hope Elizabeth," her father had gruffly insisted when she had complained. "You need to be ready to take your place in society, to know how to act. Case closed." Case closed. The case had always been closed when it came to Hope's opinions. So she had attended the dancing class under protest, tripping over her own feet, and with her hair often falling out of her hairbows. She wore her little white gloves, but she had drawn little puppet faces on the fingertips for comic relief, much to Miss Panarelli's obvious dismay.

Meridith, on the other hand, had always been the picture of

charm and grace. She learned the dances in a flash, always knew exactly what to say in every social situation, and loved to dress up. She was smart as a whip, and had decided at a very early age that she would determinedly pursue a career in law. And that was the key to *her* disapproval of the dance class.

She had no intention of smiling coyly at boys to entice them to ask her to dance. She had no intention of sitting on the sidelines or being a "supportive" wife to a husband's up-and-coming career. She wanted her own career, and she didn't want to play games about it. She wanted to lead, she didn't want to follow.

While the other girls had fought over the eligible and handsome young heirs in the dance class, Hope and Meridith had shared the good-natured Henry. As a threesome, they had danced around the floor of the cherry-paneled ballroom, "One, two, three, one, two, three," stepping on each other's toes, and laughing at Hope's tendency to have two left feet.

The memory made Hope smile.

"Good old Henry the Fourth. Whatever happened to him, Mer?"

"Geez, you *are* out of touch, pet lady! He just won a congressional seat, out in the western suburbs. Don't you ever read a paper?"

"Not if I can get away with it. And you saw my picture—can you blame me?"

Meridith gave an exaggerated sigh. "So are you going to tell me about el hunko in the paper or am I going to have to put a detective on it and find out for myself?"

She told her.

"Whew! Hope. What a story. But Noah Brandywine has such a good reputation, you know. Hardworking, generous to causes, fair with employees and the union. Are you *sure* this is true?"

Hope felt a squeeze in her heart. How she wished it wasn't true. But she had seen the animals—and the bags.

"I've got to follow it up, Meridith. Tell me what I should do."

They discussed the organizations that Hope should contact, while Hope took notes.

"Thanks for the information and support, my friend," she said softly.

"Whatever I can do, I'm here, Hope," Meridith answered. "And I'll see you next week. I have an appointment to bring Priscilla in for a checkup and to get her nails clipped."

"I'm going to clip her nails again?" Hope complained good naturedly. "When are you going to learn to do that yourself? That poodle gets more attention than most children I know."

"I don't even do my own nails, Hope honey. French poodles are delicate creatures, you know. And Priscilla is my baby."

"As long as I don't have to give her a french manicure, I suppose I should just count myself ahead. And what am I checking her over for?"

"Hmmm. I hadn't considered a french manicure, but now that you've mentioned it . . ."

"Forget it."

"Some friend. I'm concerned about her diet. Her coat seems rougher."

Hope laughed. "Maybe she just needs a deep conditioning treatment, Mer. Remember, she's a poodle, not a fashion model. But I'll check her over, I promise."

"Keep in touch with your progress about the kisser. That picture really looked promising. Though you could do with a make over, Hope Elizabeth. It wouldn't kill you to come with me for one day to the salon. It's no affront to your personhood to look your best, you know. Hair, nails—a facial."

"You're wasting your time. And for someone who bills so much for an hour, Meridith, I'm surprised you'd bother. You've never won the salon argument. Give it up; it's a lost cause."

"Hmmm. Perhaps I've never had motivation on my side before. You know, I always wanted to meet that Noah Brandywine. Are you sure we can't share?"

"Forget it, Counselor. Get back to work."

She broke the connection and looked down at her notes. Her stomach was in knots. Her emotions felt like they were in a whirling blender. She might want to shoot Noah Brandywine, but she sure didn't want to share him. Even with Meridith. Especially with Meridith. Where was Henry the Fourth when you needed him?

She picked up the phone again and began to call the organizations on her list.

It was a typical day at Hope's Haven. She spayed two cats, patched up a beagle who had seen the worst end of a fight with a Siamese, did surgery to set a badly broken hind leg on a German Shepherd, and prevented and/or cured a long list of patients from distemper, infestation by worms and other parasites, and bladder infections. She kept her mind firmly on her animal practice, and firmly off the makeup magnate because even the thought of him (in addition to the thought of her reaction to him) made her mad enough to spit.

In between visits, she fielded calls investigating the complaints that she had lodged about the animal abuse, and explained the necessity of a weight reduction diet to the owner of a seriously obese Golden Retriever. She also checked and coddled Georgia's thriving puppies, reporting each one's weight and individual physical characteristics to her owner, who was anxiously awaiting his release from the hospital.

Through the course of the morning, she drank four lukewarm cups of coffee, complaining about each one, then scarfed a greasy burger that Manny brought her when he arrived after school.

The flowers arrived just as she and Manny were closing the clinic for the day. Hope was looking ahead to a miserable night of trying to balance the clinic's books, attempting to squeeze the necessary funds to feed all the additional rescuees out of an already ridiculously pulverized budget.

Tattoos and sweatshirts just weren't going to pay these bills. She needed an influx of cash money. She needed to deal with the problem of Noah Brandywine. She needed to assure that no more animals would be needlessly harmed. The thoughts gave her a headache.

So when the delivery girl pulled the colorful flower van into the smooth-as-glass driveway and presented her with an extravagant bouquet of wildflowers, she was preoccupied and surprised.

"Oh, they are gorgeous," she whispered, burying her head in the wide variety of colorful blooms. Had she forgotten her birthday?

Manny stood behind her in the doorway, watching her with a thoughtful look on his young face.

She opened the card that was attached to the vase.

"I thought you might like wildflowers. Noah."

She plopped down on the clinic steps as the flower van pulled away. Flowers from Noah. Flowers from the man whose touch made her melt, and whose incriminating plastic bags were floating in the river. Her stomach lurched treacherously. The headache increased.

"It just can't be him, Manny," she whispered desolately.

Manny took the flowers from her arms, watching her.

"Come on," he said, wisely refraining from making any comments. "Get over to the house and relax for a bit. You look like shit. I'll carry the flowers."

She did as he said. He placed the flowers on the bookshelf in her living room, and glanced at her before he left.

"You take it easy, Hope. And don't get carried away. People ain't always what they seem."

"Aren't. Aren't always what they seem." Her voice trailed off.

"Whatever. But nobody's going to hurt you, Doc. Nobody." He squared his chin.

"Maybe it's too late for that." She thought of the taste of Noah's lips, the way he smiled, the way he made her feel. Her heart could simply not believe that he was involved in the testing mess. But facts were facts, and her heart was probably making her less than objective.

She looked over at the flowers, and her heart felt pulled in two.

"I wish we knew for sure."

"You've turned the facts in to the authorities, Hope, and they listened. We'll get the truth, even if we don't like it."

He looked over at the flowers. "They're just flowers, Doc."

Just flowers. Just my heart.

Hope nodded, sitting down on the couch and giving in to the fatigue she felt. "I know, Manny. I just feel . . . beaten."

"It'll be okay, Doc," he said almost to himself, as he left her on the couch, shutting the door behind him.

But he didn't, in truth, know if it would ever be okay. And he didn't really have the slightest bit of confidence in the authorities to ferret out the truth, especially if they were up against the giant machine of Brandywine Beauty Products.

He reached in his pocket, feeling the two crumpled hundred dollar bills that Noah had handed him a couple of days earlier. A plan began to form in his mind.

He wished he could share it with Hope, but he knew that would be a bad idea. Her first reaction would be to protect him, to keep him safe. And this was not about protecting him. It was about protecting her. Somebody had to do it. For sure, she had been there to protect him when he had needed it. His turn, that was all.

He climbed on his bicycle and peddled away as fast as his eighteen-year-old legs could carry him.

Noah Brandywine caught himself whistling on his way to work on Monday. He felt great.

Well, not exactly great. His back felt distinctly like he had been put on the rack and tortured a bit. His elbow ached. Why exactly did they call it the funnybone, anyway? He stuck his arm out the window of the Jaguar and stretched it. He would not want to list falling out of trees as a resumé item, or to make it a habit. But he would heal, he supposed. And other than the minor physical woes, he felt exuberant.

Hope Highfield was the reason. He thought of her flashing smile and her quirky sense of humor. He thought of the way her eyes lit up when she laughed, and how deep and thoughtful she looked when she listened to him. She really listened.

He felt butterflies in his stomach at the thought of her. He sped down the road along the river, aiming for a new and productive week at Brandywine Beauty Products. The sun was shining, making the river sparkle in the early morning light.

He grinned. Noah Brandywine was thinking of sparkling rivers and sunlight. He had a 10 A.M. meeting with the union heads this morning, sure to be a battle extraordinaire. On any other occasion, he would have jumped out of bed like a gladiator with a mission—focused, determined, on guard. But a tiny slip of a woman with hair that tended to have a mind of its own, and bare brown legs that made his mouth water, had changed all that. See what love could do to you?

Abruptly, his foot pounded the brakes of his beloved Jag. Tires screeched to a halt as the car stopped. Frozen on the side of the road, he closed his eyes and attempted to swallow.

Love? Had he said love?

There were no witnesses. He hadn't even spoken aloud. But the thoughts inside his head had been loud and clear. *See what love can do to you?*

He had spent his life avoiding it. He had seen the results of his mother's one disastrous love affair with a man who had left her penniless, with a small child. He had seen how love could cloud your thoughts, warp your judgement, and then steal your dignity and your self-esteem.

He had loved his mother with his every breath as a kid. He had watched her work herself to an early grave trying to provide for him, to give him a better life. He had watched her grieve for the man that she had loved, never accepting the fact that he had left and would never return. Noah had hated that.

He had learned to fight for success: in school, in business, in life. He had learned to be strong. And he had avoided the whole idea of love like the plague.

See what love can do to you?

He thought of his mother's tired face. But then he thought of Hope's laughing eyes, the way she had spoken to him over the restaurant table, the way she had felt in his arms.

Love didn't have to destroy you. It all depended on who you decided to love, that was all. He put the car into gear again, and pulled out onto the road.

He could love wisely. Hope was an intelligent woman. She would agree. Their relationship could grow in a carefully controlled way, that would encompass both of their lives. He smiled again, anxious to see her.

He had ordered a bouquet to be delivered to the clinic; wildflowers that were just like her, natural and splashed with color. She'd love them.

With his earlier exuberance restored, he made the last turn toward Brandywine Beauty Products. No more thoughts about sunshine and wildflowers. Time to focus on the union contract. His mind slipped into work mode. Immediately following the union presentation, he had a meeting with Research about the new products being developed. Then lunch with the advertising executives who were coming in from Manhattan to pitch the new campaign they had created for the fall launch.

In the afternoon he was meeting with some local politicians about a zoning complaint near his Philadelphia warehouse. He could handle this agenda, and then he would go see Hope. His body tightened again at the thought.

He pulled into the well-paved, well-landscaped driveway of Brandywine Beauty Products. He swallowed hard.

A small crowd had gathered by the door. Several were carrying signs. *PETA hates Brandywine Beauty*, said one. People for the Ethical Treatment of Animals, he knew that group. *The SPCA will get you for this* said another in bold black print. A news van was pulling into the driveway behind him.

What was this, instant replay? He had been sure that the animal testing issue had been laid to rest as far as Brandywine Beauty Products was concerned. He had been through this before. There was no way he was going to let the media dredge up old issues just to sell papers. It had cost him a lot to get his trucks rolling after the first time.

He parked his car in his usual spot and strode purposefully toward the crowd. He would not avoid them, he would bring the matter to a head.

"People, people" he said in his calm, public voice. The cameramen had scrambled from their van and ran his way, portable cameras bouncing haphazardly on their shoulders. He smiled a welcoming smile and waved to the crew.

"I'm not sure what brings you here this morning, but I can

assure you that you are too late. As far as the issue of ethical animal testing, Brandywine Beauty Products has been exonerated, as I knew it would be. Dr. Highfield and I have discussed the misunderstanding, and have put it behind us. Now if you'll just excuse me, it's time for me to get to work."

"Well, Mr. Brandywine," came the high-pitched voice of a reed thin reporter with frizzy black hair, "You may have put it behind you, but it looks like it's going to stab you in the back. Complaints were lodged this morning with PETA, the SPCA, and the County Health Department that charge you with unethical experimentation, as well as illegal disposure of test animals. I have a feeling that you are going to be arrested by the end of the day. So what do you think of that?"

There was silence in the crowd.

Noah put up a reassuring hand.

"Whatever the problem, we will solve it. This is simply a miscommunication. I'm sure that Dr. Highfield will be able to put this issue to rest."

The crowd buzzed.

Noah felt sweat begin to drip down the back of his shirt.

The frizzy headed man spoke again. "You must think you're a better kisser than you are, Mr. Brandywine."

The crowd laughed.

"We all saw the paper with you and the Doc. You gave it your best try, but it didn't work. Dr. Highfield isn't putting this to rest. She's the one who called in the complaints this morning.

Noah Brandywine opened his mouth to speak, but nothing came out. Hope? Hope had called in the complaints? He felt like he had been kicked in the stomach.

See what love can do to you?

The words were echoing in his head as the building door opened and Frank, his security chief, strode through the crowd accompanied by two guards.

Without a word, he took Noah by the arm and led him swiftly through the door. Once inside the quiet lobby, he heard the click as the guard locked the door behind him.

"Buzzards." Frank grunted. "We'll just keep them out until we get answers to this thing."

The elevator took them soundlessly to the top floor. They walked through the reception area and into Noah's office, shutting the door behind them.

"What were you thinking of, Noah, staying in contact with that tree-hugging nut?"

Noah sat down hard in his chair, trying to concentrate. What was he thinking of? What exactly . . . had he been thinking of?

The phone lights were blinking like crazy. He stood up, crossed the office, and looked out into the reception area. His new assistant was flipping from line to line like a pro. "No comment at this time, sir, I'm sure this will all be cleared up soon." "Thank you for calling, but we do not have anything to say at this time. We are as surprised as you are." The instant she hung up a line, the light blinked again. The rest of the media had joined the parade. Bad news travels fast, it seemed.

How could Hope have done this? He thought of the smell of her, the feel of her in his arms. How could she not believe in him?

Behind him, Frank hung up the phone.

"Big problem this time, boss. They're all saying where there's smoke there's fire. The trucks are being halted at the distribution centers, and rumor has it, tomorrow's political cartoon in the New York Times features yours truly."

"I just can't believe it. I'm not responsible for any experimentation on animals. Why would she do this?"

Frank shook his head in disgust. "What's come over you, man? This is business. Your empire is about to tumble, and you have hearts and flowers in your eyes. You've been played for a sucker, Noah. Geez, I don't even know what kind of damage control this is going to take. We're going to have to cut that broad off at the knees."

"No. Leave her alone. There has to be an answer to this, and I'll find it myself."

Frank shook his head again, his brow creased in anger. "You don't look like you could find your way out of a paper bag. But it's your funeral, boss. Call me when you wake up. I'll be in my office."

With long strides, he disappeared out the door.

Noah sat staring out the large glass window for a few moments, watching the river run by. On the bank across the river, he could see the northern grassy part of Hope's Haven, looking green and peaceful. Peaceful. Did she realize the havoc she was creating for him? Did she care?

Grabbing the phone directory, he searched for the number for Hope's office, committing it to memory. He wanted to talk to her, to hear her concerns from her own lips. He dialed.

After four rings, her answering machine responded.

"You have reached Dr. Hope Highfield at Hope's Haven. If you are a media maniac, no time to talk today. If you have a pet with a problem, come on over. If you are my father, no need to say I told you so. If you are Noah Brandywine, take a hike."

He'd been tried and convicted without a defense, he thought. What had happened between last night and this morning? One way or another, he was going to figure it out. But first, he had to put out the fires at Brandywine Beauty Products.

The buzzer sounded on his desk. "Union guys are here, Mr. Brandywine, and they aren't wearing their happy faces," his assistant said into the intercom.

"Put them in the conference room. I'll be right there."

The buzzer rang again. "Carl Sendrick from personnel is here."

"Send him in."

The door opened quickly. "Four new employees are being processed this morning, boss," the little man said quietly. "Still want to give them the Brandywine pep talk as usual?"

It was his trademark, a sincere welcome to people of all levels who joined the Brandywine ranks. He had spent a lifetime building this dream. He wasn't going to let it get washed away without a fight.

"Eleven A.M." he said in the most positive voice he could muster. "Business as usual."

He could see the respect in Carl's eyes as he nodded his approval. "We'll be ready."

His private line rang. "Good morning, Handsome," Cheryl's voice dripped over the line. Obviously, she had forgiven him. Also obviously, she had not heard about the recent troubles at Brandywine. Cheryl avoided trouble.

"Good morning, Cheryl," he said in a neutral tone. "I'm a bit busy today."

"I just wanted to let you know that I forgive you for your rudeness the other night. I'm not used to being forgotten. But I've decided to give you the chance to make it up to me. Dinner tonight?"

He ran a hand over his brow. He didn't need more trouble. He had all he could handle already. "Sorry, Cheryl. This just isn't a good time for me."

Her voice sounded icy. "Do you mean tonight? Or do you mean ever?"

Three days ago, he had found her entertaining, an enjoyable companion. Now she grated on his nerves like an out of tune violin string. What was happening to him?

"I'm sorry, Cheryl. It isn't going to work out. It's just me. It's nothing personal."

"It couldn't be more personal," the icy tone barked back, and then the connection was broken.

He sighed. He was a sick man. He was turning down the beautiful Cheryl, the classy and society proven ice princess, because he couldn't get a muddy, mussy haired little brunette out of his mind. Hope was an impulsive, emotional hothead who was trying to bring down his business in a single blow.

Later, he would figure it all out. Later, he would go see that woman who had gotten under his skin and do whatever it took to put her fears to rest. Because he knew he was innocent. And he also knew that he wasn't going to stop thinking about her, no matter how she ignored him.

Suddenly he felt a little like Billie the Goat with his unrequited love. *Naaah! Baaah!* He pushed the thought aside. Right now he had a business to run, and a reputation to save.

He stood up, took a deep power breath, and went to tackle the union guys.

Later, he thought resolutely, he'd tackle Hope Highfield. And he wasn't sure if he'd kiss her or throttle her.

Chapter Seven

Hope's day flew by, a usual occurrence when her schedule was packed. It was close to five by the time she realized that Manny had not shown up after school.

It sure hadn't taken long for the news of her complaints to PETA and the FDA to leak to the press. Almost with the speed of light, nosy reporters had been on the phone and on her doorstep. But she was taking no enjoyment in this. She simply wanted the abuse to stop, and she trusted the agencies now involved would do their job.

The fact that Brandywine was obviously involved cut like a knife wound. She took no joy in turning Noah in. She had simply done what had to be done to stop the abuse.

More than anything in the world, she wanted to forget about Noah Brandywine, and the fact that he had lied to her. She wanted to forget that she had been so vulnerable, so easily swayed, so pliant in his arms.

When the last client had left, and the chores were done, Hope was tired but antsy. She went in back to her apartment and changed into running clothes.

Hope had a few favorite routes that she liked to travel when she was jogging. The route she took today took her around the perimeter of her property, on a well worn path that followed the fence line on one long side, and then returned along the riverbank. Each loop was a mile. Today she jogged with concentration, finished her run, and returned to the clinic.

And like in a bad dream, she saw Noah's silver Jag parked at her office door. It was empty.

Where was he?

She looked around the property, but it looked deserted. Not even the cats had come to greet her. As she crossed to the office door, she noticed that it was partly open. She stepped inside.

He was sitting on the ugly orange vinyl couch that took up one entire wall of her waiting room. His suit was charcoal, well pressed and obviously expensive. He was staring straight ahead, his face expressionless.

In front of him, Billie the Goat sat on her haunches like a large dog, staring right at him. Three cats were lined up on the counter, not moving a whisker.

"You're back," he said quietly, not moving his head.

"What are you doing here?" She could hear her own heart hammering, and wondered if it was audible in the room.

"Sitting. Just sitting." He moved his eyes slightly, and as soon as he did, the goat moved closer. He let out his breath.

"Hope, please. You may shoot me, you may pole-axe me, but please, please, save me from this goat right now before I have a heart attack."

Hope opened the office door. "Billie, scat," she said firmly. "Go check the pups."

The goat left with a wiggle, only looking over her shoulder one time.

He relaxed.

"I had to come and talk, no matter what. I had to clear this up. The reporters, the FDA, those wild PETA people, they are all sure that you are making complaints against me again. I told them we had talked this out, that there had to be some mistake, but—"

"There is no but, Noah. More evidence has come to light, and I'm sure now that Brandywine is involved. I didn't want it to be true." Her voice broke. "But—" Hope reached over to the desk and pulled a clump of river-stained plastic bags from the drawer. "There are these, Noah," she said, thrusting them at him. "Manny found these floating in the river with the last batch of patients."

He stared at the Brandywine Beauty bags. He couldn't believe what he saw.

"But it's still not true. I'll even stare down a goat to prove to you it's not true, Hope. I have never done anything illegal at Brandywine."

"There's a fine line between illegal and unethical in these issues, Noah. I realize that testing is allowed. As much as I hate it, I realize that animals are bred and used for testing of products and drugs in this society. But there are laws regarding how that is done, regarding pain, and suffering. And disposal." Her voice broke again.

His voice was strained. "Hope, I will say one last time. I have *never* allowed *any* animal testing at Brandywine Beauty Products. This company has been my life. I have build it from scratch and have watched it grow."

He thought of the trucks being returned to the distribution centers, the employees who would lose their jobs if the production lines shut down.

"This company is important not only to me. It's important to my employees too. People's lives are at stake here."

He thought of his missed meeting this afternoon, having to forfeit his usual welcome to two more new employees, because of the emergency conference with his attorneys. In so many ways, his rhythm was being interrupted, the things that he took pride in were being compromised. How many ways would his company suffer because of the time and energy needed to build a defense? And for what? What had he done wrong?

"While it may be true that we have used the data that has been collected in the past by other scienfic agencies to be sure that our products are safe, we have never initiated any tests ourselves. I swear this to you." He stood to leave.

"But the evidence."

"I don't know about any evidence. I only know that sooner or later, a person has to trust their instincts, their feelings, more than any evidence."

He looked at the slender, sweaty woman who stood in front of him. He should hate her. He should be filled with rage for the havoc she had wrought. And yet, he was just filled with sadness, for what might have been. He had to fight the urge to reach out for her, to pull her into his arms. But that, he was sure, would never happen again. He turned and walked out the door.

"It'll all come to light, sooner or later," Meridith said on the phone later that evening. "PETA is investigating, and the FDA. You should just put it out of your mind for now, Hope. You are worrying too much. Saturday night, I want you to come with me to a charity event being hosted by the city. I'm being given an award for my pro bono work regarding the licensing of daycares."

"You, Meridith? You're doing pro bono work?"

"Ah, you of little faith! You don't corner the market in the "good deeds" category, Hope Elizabeth. Lately, I've done plenty of free work, including, mind you, Hope's Haven and your little problem."

Meridith's voice sounded light, but Hope could detect the hurt underneath.

"No offense meant, Meridith. And I'll be glad to go and see you get your accolades."

A stuffy city event with dinner and dancing was the last thing she wanted to do, but she wouldn't have turned down Meridith for the world.

"And guess who called? Remember Henry the Fourth from

dancing school? Well, the new congressman just called to say he'll be attending. He asked about you, by the way. Maybe we can all dance, like old times.

Hope chuckled. "That'd be a sight." She thought about chubby Henry. It had been years since she had seen him. "It'll be good to see him again."

"Maybe you two will hit it off," said Meridith in her usual manipulating way. "After giving it much thought, I think you are just right for each other. And he sounds—cuter—on the phone."

"Whatever," said Hope, laughing at her friend. "But I wouldn't select the wedding invitations yet, Ms. Fixup. I'm becoming more and more of a committed bachelorette every day."

"We'll see about that. Or maybe I'll take him for myself!" said the lawyer lightly, as she hung up the phone.

There was no answer at Manny's foster home, when Hope tried to call a few minutes later. This didn't surprise her in the least, as the family always seemed to be in constant motion as they ran to baseball games, ballet lessons, and school conferences for the many children who came and went in their care.

"Hi, Manny," she said into the phone, leaving a message on the tape. "This is Hope. Missed you today, but I'm sure you were busy. Just let me know your schedule this week, so I can get some coverage if you aren't going to be here. Thanks. Bye."

She kept her voice light. She did not want the nagging worry she felt about Manny to grow out of proportion. Next she called the woman who came and worked occasionally when things were extremely busy, to see if she was available.

"Hi, Frances," she said when the senior citizen answered the phone in her perky voice. "I'm frantic this week. Do you want to come in?"

"Glory be, I'd love to. Can use the extra yarn money, for sure. I'm in the middle of crocheting a most unusual afghan pattern, and it's taking twice the yarn I'd estimated. What a dilemma.

"I'll come over tomorrow morning, and we can work out the schedule for the rest of the week. Warn the goat."

"She'll be on her best behavior."

"Like that's something to brag about. I will bring a new recipe for goat stew. That will keep her thinking."

It was a standing feud. Frances loved *all* the animals, and tended them with care. She even secretly loved Billie, Hope knew. But she would never forgive her for eating an irreplaceable ball of yarn in a unique color of clay red. Billie would be in the goathouse forever for that.

In the morning, Hope had to face the fact that she had not heard back from Manny.

Frances arrived at 9 A.M. as promised, her bluish grey hair coiffed like a mushroom, her tiny body sporting a long, flowing blue skirt, a tye-dyed T-shirt in rainbow hues, and a pair of purple high-topped sneakers.

"New shoes, Frances?" Hope said with a grin, looking up from the kitten whose eye she had been irrigating.

"Have to keep up with the times, Doc," she said determinedly, plopping down her overflowing bag of yarn and partly finished afghan. "And these have good arches, lots of support. These can clear high buildings with a single leap, faster than a speeding bullet . . ."

"I get the picture. I think I need a pair of those, too."

"No doubt about it. Now what's this about you and this Noah creature across the river. I saw your picture in the paper, heard the news about the animal problem. I'm sure the media has been hounding you to death."

On cue, the phone rang. Frances picked it up without missing a beat. "Hope's Haven. This is Frances . . . Yes . . . No . . . No comment. I appreciate that you are interested. Would you like to contribute to Hope's Save the Animals Fund? If you could give me your credit card number and the amount, I can take care of it from here. Hello? Hello?"

She hung up the phone.

"My oh my, he hung up. Wasn't so interested in the animals after all, I suppose."

She grinned, her face wrinkling into a million lines, like a well-used piece of tin foil. "I'm sure I can handle the media, Doc."

Hope laughed out loud.

"You just take care of the animals, and that Noah."

"The animals I can handle." Hope returned her attention to the kitten. "But handling Noah Brandywine is another thing entirely."

Hope had finished a grueling day when the evening edition of the paper arrived. Frances had gone home with the promise to return in the morning. Manny hadn't arrived after school, and another phone call to his foster home hadn't located him. Where was Manny?

While there had been no new emergencies, the struggle to treat the already full list of patients kept her busy all day. Three of the rescued kittens had lost their fight for life. They had been the ones who had shown signs of severe skin testing that had been left untreated, and the ensuing infections had been too much for their little bodies to bear.

While Hope knew that using animals for testing was a common practice in many areas of research, it tore at her heart to see the results. In fact, the FDA insisted that many human products with medicinal value be fully tested before approval. But the FDA, with the Federal Food, Drug and Cosmetic Act (FD&C), now had strict rules for those companies whose research included testing products and medicines on animals for product safety. Those rules monitored the pain level, the types of tests allowed, and the humane treatment of those animals both during and after the experiments. Painful, tortuous death was not allowed.

Many organizations helped to bring these issues into the public consciousness, including PETA.

Cosmetic companies such as Brandywine had no legal need to test their products. And many cosmetic companies, again such as Brandywine, greatly increased sales by their public pronouncements of being "cruelty free" and "not tested on animals."

But why would Noah test his products so cavalierly, in direct opposition to his own advertising claims? Legally, he could test products if he wished. Ethically, there were ways to do it that would be publicly acceptable, even if against Hope's own ethics. Why risk it all in such a flagrant way? It didn't make sense.

Hope restocked the medicine shelf in her office and pulled the files needed for the next day's appointments. Manny had not shown up or called. It simply wasn't like him. The nagging apprehension in her stomach was rapidly turning to worry. He had been so upset about Brandywine. He had felt so frustrated about the situation. Was his disappearance linked to it?

She picked up the phone and called his home a third time.

"Hi, Hope," said the usually cheerful woman in a tired voice. "Manny's not here. I was kind of hoping he was with you. He didn't come home last night, and school called and said he wasn't there today. He's usually such a darn good kid, I give him the benefit of the doubt. But this is too long. He's gone-too long. I'm going to have to call social services."

"Yes, I think you should," said Hope calmly, though her nerves were jangling, and she was the exact opposite of calm. "And call me if you hear anything, okay?"

Manny was definitely missing.

She put the phone on the hook, picked up the newspaper and opened it up. The big black headline screamed out at her.

DO YOU KNOW SOMEONE WHO IS MISSING? UNIDEN-TIFIED BODY FOUND

For the first time in her entire life, Hope Elizabeth Highfield passed out—stone cold. Her legs buckled, and down she went, paper clutched in her hand. She missed the soft cushions of the couch by a good twelve inches and hit the tile floor of her office with a resounding thud.

A good ten minutes had passed when Noah found her there. After looking for her at her house, he had followed the path to her office, where the light was still lit. The first glimpse of her, collapsed like a rag doll on the floor, put him into a panic. In two long strides he reached her, scooped her up, and placed her gently on the couch. Her eyes were fluttering as he grabbed a small towel and ran it under the faucet. Returning to her, he stroked her forehead with the cool compress.

"Hope." He heard the raspiness of his own voice and almost didn't recognize it. "Hope!" There was a feeling of panic welling up in his chest as he felt her stillness. He had begun dialing 911 when he saw her eyes begin to flutter. He froze, staring at her.

Hope blinked slowly, eyes suddenly focusing on the man kneeling beside her. Thoughts came back, flashes at first, and then the full memory of the headline about the unidentified body, and Manny's disappearance. And Noah Brandywine right here in front of her.

"Manny!" she cried, tears spilling and making instant trails down her face. "Manny!"

Frustration, anger, and fear swirled inside of her, ripping her up. Was he dead? Did it have something to do with the animal testing? Was it the fault of the man who was staring at her right now as if she had two heads?

Anger suddenly ripped through her, and she struck out at him, raised her fists, flailing at him. The blows landed ineffectually on his broad chest. He didn't try to stop her.

Noah could see the pain in her wide eyes, though he didn't know the source. He pulled her toward him, wanting to comfort her.

"Hope, Hope, what is it? What happened?" Her energy flagged, and she collapsed, her entire frame shaking in his embrace. He held her close, then felt her resistance.

"No, no," she cried, even harder. "Don't do this. Don't make me feel like this." The pain of loss and fear was lodged deep inside, her worry for Manny like a slice of a knife. Was he dead?

Like a wave, the horror threatened to overtake her once more—again she felt ready to crack into a million little pieces, held together by only a strong pair of arms.

His arms. Noah Brandywine's arms. The tears continued as she fought a war inside of herself. Why was it that this man who had caused all the problems seemed to be the only one who could comfort her? She felt tired, she felt sick.

But she had stopped shaking. Noah lowered her gently to the couch. Seeing the paper on the floor, he picked it up. The headline loomed up at him, and he instantly knew what she had assumed. But he also knew it wasn't true.

"It wasn't Manny. You thought it was Manny. Is he missing?" His words were soft, spoken into her hair, right above her ear.

The words registered. Her breath returned to normal.

"Are you certain? It wasn't Manny?" The relief swept through her like a strong spring breeze. It wasn't Manny. She could see the truth in his eyes. But also something else. Worry.

"Who was it?" she asked tentatively.

"One of my employees from the second shift. His name was John Perkins. Blonde, twenty-five, tall and thin. He was a good kid. But no chance he'd be mistaken for Manny."

"I'm—I'm sorry" she stuttered. A life had been lost. She had been so relieved about Manny, she hadn't given a thought to the young man who had died.

She sat up. "I was so afraid. He was so enraged about the latest surge of animal dumping. I was afraid he had taken it on himself to investigate. I'm so glad he isn't. . . ."

"Don't be too glad yet, Hope." His tone was deep and serious. "Manny did decide to investigate Brandywine Beauty. Evidently he applied for a maintenance job on the second shift to get into the plant. He started today with two other new employees. Normally, I meet all the hirees, but today I didn't meet him because I was tied up with the damn legal meeting concerning this attack by PETA."

He remembered his original mission. He had driven to Hope's Haven for a reason. He needed her to believe in him, desperately. "Someone's setting me up."

"Don't try to make this sound like a bad movie, Noah. Nobody is setting you up. Manny was trying to find out the truth."

"Well, he found more than his share of trouble," Noah said sadly. "That's what I came to tell you. About Manny. He was the last person to see John Perkins alive, according to plant witnesses. He was the last person to leave at the end of the shift."

"What does that mean?" Hope cried, fear again clutching her heart.

"It means that Manny is wanted for murder, Hope. The cops ran his sheet and found out he has a record as long as your arm, as a kid in New York. He took the job under false pretenses, and only hours later, a man was found dead. They are investigating his prior gang ties, drugs—"

"No!" Hope cried. "That's all in the past."

"Maybe to you, Hope, but not to the cops. They are looking all over for him, and it looks like he's run. That was my main reason for coming here, Hope, to find Manny. Do you know where he is?"

"No," she whispered, fear entwining itself around her heart. "But I know he wouldn't do something like that. I just know."

He stared at her silently. His pulse was hammering. She just knew. She just knew Manny was innocent of murder.

Just like she knew that Noah was guilty of breaking the laws of humane treatment to animals. He tried to swallow but couldn't. What would he give for belief like that? What would he give to have Hope Highfield's trust?

But he didn't have it. She blamed him for the whole blasted thing, and there wasn't anything he could do about it. He stood, waving off the sadness.

"If you hear from him, Hope, better let the authorities know. They are looking for him. It'll look better if he turns himself in."

"But he's innocent!"

"He left a life of crime before, Hope. He ran away from the gangs. It sure looks like he's run again."

"There's an explanation."

"For his sake, I hope you are right. But somebody plugged that poor young guy and tossed him into the river. And Manny has disappeared. It sure looks like guilt to the authorities."

"But maybe something has happened to him, too. Did anyone think of that?"

"I did, Hope. I mentioned that. The police think otherwise."

Her stubborn chin came forward, and her eyes blazed.

"We don't have all the facts. Looks can be deceiving."

"Tell me something I don't know," he said under his breath as he turned his back to her and walked toward the door.

"Noah," she called softly.

He stopped and turned, seeing tears pooled in her brown eyes. With two strides, he was back to her, wrapping his arms around her, holding her close.

Held close against his chest, Hope closed her eyes and let his warmth envelop her. Safe. She felt safe. The tears began to fall.

He held her there, as her shoulders shuddered and she cried herself out. He stroked her hair with one hand and gently rubbed her back with the other. He'd like to get his hands on the people who had caused her this pain. But at the moment, all he could offer was his love and support. And the love she didn't want. She didn't really trust him. So he'd settle for the support.

He didn't speak until the sobs had subsided, and she was quiet in his arms.

"We'll find the answers, Hope, and we'll find Manny." His voice caught, and he surprised himself at how much he wanted his words to be true. And how much he wanted her to believe in him.

She pulled away, and composed herself. "Sorry for the outburst. So many feelings. Send me the cleaning bill if I've wrecked another shirt."

He smiled softly and wiped a tear from under her eye with his thumb.

"Don't worry about it. I have it all under control. I bought a hundred shares of Brooks Brothers stock today. Might as well have a piece of the profits from increased sales."

He put a finger under her chin and raised her head so he could look into her eyes.

"I'm a financial wizard, remember? Even though a poorly dressed one at times."

She had to smile back. He had that effect on her. Even in

the midst of dismay and worry, he just made the world feel right.

"Ok," he said. "Have you had dinner yet?"

"I was just going to cook." She paused. "Want to stay and help? And eat?"

His stomach flipped. There was nothing he'd like better.

"Sure. What are we making?"

She took his hand and led the way out. When they reached her little kitchen, she motioned him to a stool. Opening the refrigerator, she stuck her head inside and began throwing things on the counter in front of him. "Vegetarian surprise. Start chopping."

He swallowed hard, but he didn't dare complain. Where was the meat? The potatoes?

When in doubt, follow directions. He chopped.

He chopped green peppers. He chopped string beans. Hope busied herself setting up a rice cooker and making some long grain brown rice. She made exotic iced tea. He chopped tomatoes. He chopped celery and carrots. A hidden talent, this chopping. The onion was a challenge. His eyes were tearing as he worked the knife. He had heard that onions can make a grown man cry. That may be true. But as the onion was reduced to little chunks, and his eyes misted over, he also knew a strange and wonderful emotion at this simple task, working alongside Hope.

The vegetables were thrown into Hope's waiting pot and set to simmer. It looked awful. It smelled like heaven.

"You are going to eat this?" he said, standing over the pot and stirring like he knew what he was doing. "I think you've been hanging around that stupid goat too long."

Hope looked at him with a smirk. "If I was a suspicious person, I would think that this was the first time you ever did this. Don't you cook?"

He looked horrified. "Of course I cook!" He lowered his voice. "I microwave."

She started laughing.

"In containers. From the gourmet restaurant in town. I pick up containers of delicious and expensive meals made by Andre the chef, and then I bring them home and nuke them to death. It works for me."

"Well, you will love this."

"That's for you to say. I am used to beef. Or pork chops. Even a goat burger would be good."

She reached into the refrigerator again and came out with a hunk of cheese; then she grabbed a loaf of fresh-baked bread off the counter. "I buy the bread. No time to bake. But I like to make the rest. Believe me, you will like this."

They sat at the little table a few minutes later, putting Hope's "Veggie Surprise" over brown rice, munching on little squares of imported cheese and ripping off hunks of fresh, soft bread. It was, without a doubt, the best meal of his life.

They talked as they ate, about their childhoods, about their hopes, about their dreams. For a few magic moments, they put the stresses and worries of the day out of their minds.

Hope basked in the intimacy, especially when he reached over and picked up a piece of cheese, offering it up to her lips, feeding her. Her eyes opened wide as she took it, a warmth flooding her face as she reached and did the same for him.

They took their time over the meal, both savoring each second. They ate every single bite. When they finally finished, Hope reached for her napkin to wipe the last drop of juice from her lips. He caught her hand, holding the napkin, and kissed her gently on the lips.

Hope's Veggie Surprise. He sighed. He would remember the taste forever. Then even more gently, he wiped her lips with the napkin.

Now *this* was fine dining!

They cleaned up together, and Noah could see how tired Hope was from her long and eventful day.

"I'm going to go now, Hope, so you can rest. But I'll be in touch. Whatever happens, I'll be in touch."

She nodded and watched him go, praying silently that when he got in touch, it would be with good news about Manny.

Chapter Eight

Society was just not kind when it came to suspicions of an ex-gang member/foster home teenager who had been seen in the vicinity of a violent crime on the night in question.

Hope's spirit was heavy the next day as the gossip spread. The press and general public appeared to be ready to lynch the young man.

Didn't several years of hard work mean anything to people? Didn't the honor roll, a good work history, and a clean record count for something? Evidently not.

The public had judged Manny Perez guilty. No wonder he had run, Hope thought angrily. She would not let go of the conviction that he had not committed the crime. But where was he?

At 4:00 P.M. Hope tended to her last patient, and was ready for some peace and quiet.

"Big doings at the National Pharmaceuticals factory across the river and up a piece. Traffic was awful. News vans and such," the farmer said casually as he was getting ready to leave.

Hope's pulse began to race. The National Pharmaceuticals factory? What was going on there? Could they be involved in this mess in some way? It was time to find out.

She said goodby to the ruddy-faced farmer and grabbed her purse.

"I'm going to go check it out," she said in a rush to a baffled Frances. "I'll be back."

"Okay," the woman said, nodding her bluish-gray head and waving a knitting needle. "Take your time. I'll stay right here. But if you're not back by 6:30, I'm turning on the tube to watch the "Wheel of Fortune" and "Jeopardy." Can't miss Vanna. Hey, Doc," Frances called to the swinging door. "You're still wearing your lab coat."

The words echoed in the empty room. Hope was gone.

Hope drove her old car easily into the drive at the factory and parked at the end of the very full lot.

At the rear of the building, several vans were parked, camera equipment strapped to the top. What was such big news?

She hurried toward the crowd that had gathered by the door.

"Excuse me," "Pardon me," she said over and over as she maneuvered her way to the front of the crowd. As she neared the door, it opened and a beefy Rent-a-Cop positioned himself on the front steps.

"It's like I says before," he said in a gruff voice. "There's already a crowd inside and no one else is gonna be let in. Stand back."

He spoke importantly to the grumbling crowd. "You'll just hafta see it on the TV. It's been held up, anyways, waiting for the doctor."

His eyes scanned the crowd, and came to rest on Hope. The eyes brightened and he smiled.

"And here she is. Come, Doc. They're waitin' on you, and you know what those types are when they're in a hurry."

With an authoritarian air, he bent from his position on the

stair and grabbed the sleeve of Hope's lab coat. Her stethoscope jangled around her neck as he led her up the stone steps.

Waiting for her? She didn't have time to think, but she wanted more than anything to get inside. So without resisting, she followed the chubby man through the door.

Lights were glaring overhead and from all sides. A large wooden desk sat on a platform at the front of the room, a stately desk chair perched behind it. A backdrop that looked strangely like a wall of books was being hung in place.

"She's here," the big man barked importantly, and a few heads turned.

"Over there," said a suited woman with tight hair and a clipboard. "Makeup."

She was plopped on a stool in the corner of the room and two men with pony tails fussed over her.

"Wait," she said.

"No time to wait," one of the men barked, fluffing her hair. "No time to spare."

Her mind was racing, trying to figure out what was going on, but before she could say a word, she was propelled with gusto toward the desk.

"Ah, the doctor is here," said an older man in a black shirt and pants. He looked her up and down as if she were a side of beef. "Excellent look. Excellent."

"I have a few questions," she said to the man, who had an air of being in charge amidst the chaos of the room.

"Easy, toots," said a woman with a clipboard. "Just do your job, and you'll get paid. Sign."

It was a moment of decision. Should she take a stand and defy the woman, probably getting thrown out in the process? Or should she go along and try to find out what was happening? With great care, she signed "Frances McCay" on the line at the bottom of the form. Her receptionist would forgive her anything!

They hustled her to the desk and she found herself plopped into the chair. People were bustling all around her. Standing in the far corner of the room, a man in a baseball cap watched her with curiosity. He withdrew a thin tablet and pencil from the pocket of his denim jacket, and a digital phone from the pocket of his khaki pants. Quietly, he made a call. Then he put the phone away and got ready to write.

"Lights, camera, action," called the man in a singsong voice. "National Phamaceuticals commercial. Take one." The cameras rolled.

Hope Highfield blinked her eyes. Commercial?

There was a bustle at the door, and two men in gray suits rushed in, followed by two uniformed policemen.

"That's her!" the first one yelled, pushing his way through the crowd.

"She's a fraud! She's not an actor. She's a troublemaker for sure! That's that Dr. Hope Highfield who's been causing a stir everywhere she goes. And now here she is under false pretenses, trying to infiltrate National Pharmaeceuticals, trying to get her hands on our secret product before it hits the market. Our stock prices! Our secret campaign!"

The man was huffing and puffing so much, Hope was afraid he was going to collapse with a heart attack.

"No, seriously, I can explain," she said, standing at the desk, her stethescope dangling from her neck. "I know this seems ridiculous, but I just came to see what was going on."

"She signed a false name. She didn't write Dr. Hope Highfield," screeched the woman with the bun, waving her clipboard. "She wrote Frances McCay. Right here. I thought she was the actress from Equity."

There was a rumble in the crowd as the two policemen sandwiched her between them. One pulled out handcuffs. The other began his speech. "You have the right to remain silent . . ."

Oh boy, thought Hope with a frown. *Looks like I'm going to miss Jeopardy after all!*

In the morning, Hope lay on the cot in her jail cell and stared at the ceiling, trying to imagine shapes of animals from the many cracks in its plaster.

Nobody knows the trouble I've seen, she thought with a

grimace as she picked out an elephant on the ceiling. *Actually if you don't mind country music, jail isn't that bad.*

She was in a holding cell at the local police station. The sounds of Reba McIntyre reverberated through the walls. They hadn't been too happy with her, either, when she had demanded that her one phone call be to a bluish-gray-haired woman in purple sneakers, rudely interrupting her in the middle of the Daily Double on "Jeopardy," instead of to an attorney who could have gotten her out of this place.

But her first priority had been to the animals who were depending on her. Plus, she was desperate to see if there had been any messages from Manny. None. It had been a long night.

But then Officer Moe, one of the policemen, had eventually arrived to allow her to make a second phone call, which she placed to her attorney friend Meridith, or at least to Meridith's answering service.

"Hi, Mer! Guess who's locked up? When you are done exercising, would you please tort something or do whatever you do and get me out of here. I'm tired of eating rice cakes at the big house. Besides the fact that Manny has disappeared and I need you to help me find him. Hurry up, Mer. I owe you for this one."

Moe, shaking his head, had admonished her, "Now Doc, don't go making light of this. These are some serious charges. Seems National Pharmaceuticals has been having trouble with information leaking out of their labs, and they want to pursue this thing all the way."

Hope sighed. "Bad day all around, I guess."

"You got a hearing this morning."

"My lawyer's coming, don't worry."

"Here comes breakfast. I ordered you regular coffee with your pancakes."

"Thanks." She ate quietly until noise exploded from beyond the door.

"It's an outrage! I will have your badge! Now let her out of there!"

"But sir, she committed a crime."

"Balderdash!"

Balderdash? Hope thought, cringing at the sound of her father's irate voice. That was a good one, even for her father.

"Her hearing begins in fifteen minutes, and the judge will set bail."

"Bail? For a Highfield? You are going to be sorry for this! Henry! Do something! You are a blasted congressman, do something!"

Henry the Fourth, the Congressman? Her father had pulled out the big guns. So much for keeping a low profile.

"Well, Moe," she said to the officer who stood beside her, leaning on the bars, "it can't get much worse." But it could!

"Excuse me, Officer?" Another voice could be heard now, its tones deep and low and even.

Noah? And her father? And Henry the Fourth? How did they even hear of this?

"My name is Noah Brandywine, and I've come to arrange for the bail for Dr. Hope Highfield.

"You!" barked the elderly Highfield in an imperious voice. "You are the one who started this whole thing. You are certainly not paying her bail. I am paying her bail. My daughter was perfectly normal before she got involved with you. Never in jail a day in her life."

She could almost hear the smile in Noah's voice. "Only because she never got caught, Sir. Once Hope gets an idea in her head she's a menace on two legs."

How dare they talk about her like this?

"You may have a point there," her father chuckled. "I'm not sure they will be able to let her off for good behavior."

Three male voices were laughing, and Hope was fuming.

Noah recognized Henry. "Well, hello, Congressman Fulbraith. What's your tie in to this?"

"Old friend of the family, Noah. Hope and I grew up together. How's the racquetball game coming?" said Henry in a much more grownup voice than Hope remembered from dancing school.

"Hey," she called out, banging on the bars with her shoe.

"I'm not going to forgive any of you for this, ever. I can hear you out there."

Even Moe joined in the laughter, and Hope threw him a disgusted look.

But then another voice was heard as an additional person evidently walked into the office.

"Good morning, my name is Meridith Morrison, and I am counsel for Dr. Hope Highfield. I would like to confer with my client and then I would like to arrange for her bail."

"Wow," said the young officer at the desk. "We've never had a fight over who was getting to pay the bail before. Out of sight."

"Mr. Highfield!" exclaimed Meridith, recognizing Hope's father. "And this looks like Noah Brandywine. I've seen your pictures. And Henry? What are you all doing here?"

"Morning headlines, Meridith. All of a sudden, this daughter of mine seems to be plastered over every paper daily." Hugh Highfield grumbled.

Hope couldn't take it anymore. "What is this, a Three Stooges Plus One Convention? Stop the chit chat and get me out of here!" she yelled.

The door opened, and all four came into sight.

"I suppose you have a good tale to explain this?" her father began.

"I did nothing. Absolutely nothing."

All four looked back and forth at each other questioningly. Finally they broke into laughter.

"I'm telling you, I'm innocent! And I don't need your condescending help. Any of you!"

"In the words of some famous person or another," her father said in his pompous tone, "Then tell it to the judge. Case closed!"

Within minutes Hope had explained her plight to the judge, who also happened to be the owner of one of the pit bulls that she had as a client, and was released on her own cognizance to face any trespassing charges that the company might pursue after the attorneys consulted.

Without a word, she turned and strode out of the station.

The whole group followed her out the door. She turned to the group as she reached the sidewalk.

"You are an insensitive bunch of cads, as far as I'm concerned." She squinted at the quartet. "And I have no idea what any of you are doing here," she said over her shoulder, and then proceeded to walk away.

Fury smoldered in her like a smoking volcano. She would walk all the way home to the clinic. They knew better than to try to stop her.

It was a long, hot walk back to Hope's Haven. She peeled off her lab coat and tied it around her waist. After a few miles, her loafered feet began to feel like they were getting blisters.

How did she get herself into these messes? She had simply wanted to know what was going on at National Pharmaceuticals. The fact that she had almost ended up as their "Poster Doc" was simply a weird coincidence. Her father had actually called a congressman. The newspaper article must have been a doozy. She smiled suddenly, thinking of Henry as a Congressman. Goofy old Henry actually looked pretty good in his three-piece suit. He was actually handsome. A looker, as Meridith would say.

It's too bad she couldn't fall for someone like that. Someone steady and kind and calm. She shook her head sadly. She would put Noah Brandywine the corporate tycoon out of her mind. Better to be alone forever than to fall in love with someone so . . . wrong.

She stopped dead in her tracks. She winced. Love? Love?

"No! I don't love that overbearing, lying, no good animal hater! I don't!"

There was the sound of a car engine approaching on the pavement behind her. She heard the well-tuned purr of the well-designed engine.

"Go away, Brandywine," she called over her shoulder, feeling a bit like a spoiled kid who was having a temper tantrum.

"Get in the car, Highfield. I will drive you home."

"You will not." She stopped and turned around, facing him, seeing his dark profile through the windshield of the Jaguar.

"You will stay away from me, and from Hope's Haven. I will get a court order if I have to."

"You don't need a court order, Hope," he said calmly, out the open window of his car. "But you may as well take a ride. I am coming to Hope's Haven. I have to—get my dog."

"Get your dog?" she said, mystified.

"Hair. You remember him? You haven't found the owner, right? So he's mine. Get in the car."

"Hair? You are going to take care of him as a pet?" She rolled her eyes.

"I will protect him within an inch of my life. Now get in the car."

"You are a bigger dope than I thought. First of all, Hair is a she. A female. You didn't even know that?"

"I didn't look," he said sheepishly. "I'm an equal opportunity pet owner. Now will you please get in the car? You look like you are melting!"

She sighed. Her feet hurt. She was hungry. She was hot. And he looked so darn good. But she didn't love him. She didn't. She would prove that to herself.

So she opened the car door and plopped herself into the car.

"Lovely outfit," he said, ramming the car into gear and taking off before she could change her mind.

"It's what's in for the jail set this year. High fashion for high bail."

"You were let out on your own cognizance. Everybody knows this is a stupid mixup. Whatever the heck you were doing, you will get off the hook."

"But you," she continued, her voice stronger, "are not off the hook. You are taking the dog. Today. The dog needs a home, and you've committed to it."

He swallowed hard. "So I did. I keep doing things I don't expect to do." With that, he slowed the Jag, pulling it off onto the shoulder of the road, turned in his seat, and in one smooth motion, pulled Hope into his arms. His arms surrounded her, and with his fingers he gently lifted her chin until she looked into his eyes.

She saw the deepness there, the tenderness, the promised passion. As she responded. As his lips met hers, a wave of wonder flowed over her, and she kissed him back with the feelings she had been suppressing. This was Noah. And she trusted him. She needed to trust him, and she truly did.

Gently, the kiss ended, and he looked into her eyes again.

"And you do trust me, Hope Highfield. Enough to kiss me. And enough to trust me with that hairy creature you call a dog! Hope," he said meekly, thinking of what he had gotten himself into. "Will you give me dog lessons? I have no idea how to care for a dog."

"This ought to be good," she said under her breath, as the Jag pulled into Hope's Haven.

She had to give him credit. He hardly even flinched when Hair bounded out the clinic door and literally wrapped herself around his legs the minute he stepped from the car. Frances followed hot on the dog's trail, brandishing a dog brush. She was wearing a bright green T-shirt with Mickey Mouse emblazoned on the front, and a pair of pink spandex leggings—and the purple sneakers.

"Get back here," she growled, as she chased the errant dog. She waved the dog brush wildly in the air. "Somebody's got to teach you some manners and make you look like a respectable member of the canine family!"

"Somebody's going to, Frances." Hope laughed, her heart feeling instantly lighter. "Old Noah here is going to adopt old Hair. What do you think of that?"

"Well, isn't that just a plain amazing idea." She looked at Noah's impeccable grooming, her eyes traveling up to his expertly styled hair. She waved the brush again.

"He may be just the one to tackle this ball of fur. I've been trying to brush her and make her look presentable all morning. Even put in a big pink bow. She ate it."

Hair burped as if on command.

"But this one," she motioned to Noah, "can share some of those gooey hair products he uses on his own head. Have her looking like a dog show winner in no time at all."

Again Hope laughed.

"Well, Hope Highfield, I wouldn't be so quick to laugh," the colorfully clad woman continued, as she began to pull Hair back to the clinic. She looked at Hope over her shoulder. "What the heck happened to you? You look like you could use some of that goo too."

"The ravages of the prison system."

Frances didn't even blink at the news. "Doesn't surprise me," she said without any reaction at all. "Doesn't surprise me at all. I'm only surprised they let you go so quick. I'm going to get this dog ready to go."

Hair, two cats, Gretchen the Dog, and Mickey Mouse disappeared into the clinic door.

"You're taking the dog, Noah," Hope announced with finality.

"I said I would and I will," Noah said quietly. "But I need your help. Come with me. Come with me, Hope, and help me get this dog settled. I simply do not know how to do this."

Hope was touched. "Okay," she heard herself agreeing. For the dog. Just for the dog.

Gently, he raised his arms to her shoulders and pulled her close. He kissed the tip of her nose, and then his lips nuzzled the top of her head, breathing in the sweet smell of her hair. She nestled into him, feeling the strong support of the arms around her, her head resting against his chest, and feeling the rhythmic beat of his heart. She could get used to this.

"Come on. Let's go," she said gruffly.

Jaguars were not made for a crowd. Hope was scrunched up against the car door, Hair taking up far more than her 50 percent of the passenger seat, as they drove to Noah's house. At her feet rested a bag of dog supplies to get Noah started with his hairy new pet.

They crossed the river bridge and headed north. After a few miles, Noah pulled into a long drive that wound its way down toward the riverbank. His house came into view, perched right at the edge of the river, a gleaming contemporary with lots of glass. It was big and impressive, and it suited him. He pushed a few buttons, and the lower-level garage opened up soundlessly. He pulled the Jag inside. Lights automatically brightened, the door shut behind them.

"Wow!" she finally said. "More automation than Disney World!"

"It's convenient. And secure. I keep a lot of valuable information stored here, Hope. My company is in a very competitive business. And it's a dangerous world, Hope. There are bad people out there, whether you want to believe it or not. But I'm not one of them."

She wanted to be flip, to give him a fast answer, but she could not. She thought of the body that had been pulled from the river. She thought of the dead and sickly animals. She thought of Manny, still missing. It was a dangerous world. So she didn't say a word. She turned her attention to Hair instead.

"She's had all her vaccinations—distemper, rabies, heartworm, the works. So she's safe to be outside. But not running free. Pets should be kept safely under control."

They exited the car and entered the house through the garage, climbing up a few step and emerging into the kitchen.

It was white and bright and hardly looked used.

"Wow!" she exclaimed, in spite of herself. "This is awesome. And it looks brand new."

"I don't cook much." He smiled. "I can make toast and grilled cheese, and reheat a pizza. For anything else, I go out."

"It'll take her a few minutes to check things out." Hope filled a food dish and put some fresh water on the floor beside it. "Feed her now, to give her the feeling of home. Then once a day. Morning or evening, whichever you prefer."

"Does she like grilled cheese?"

Hope grinned. "As a vet, I am supposed to say that dog food is best for them—balanced and nutritious. But I'm sure an occasional grilled cheese will be fine."

"How about burnt grilled cheese? That's my specialty."

"Even better! Have an old blanket or something we can make for her bed? If she has her own space, she might take to it, and not get on the furniture until you have her trained."

"On the furniture?" Noah turned pale.

They had entered the living room. White walls, pale silver

carpet, white leather couches and a matching leather chair, silver gray accent pillows, white enamel dining room ensemble. Sitting on top of it was a feminine silk scarf. An expensive scarf. The sight of it was like the stab of a pin. This was not her world. This was Noah's world.

"Lifestyles of the Rich and Famous," she said with a forced laugh. "Hair is going to have a blast here."

Noah groaned. "I remember what that goat did to my car. What about this dog? Don't tell me my couches don't stand a chance."

With this, Hair crossed the room, jumped up into the white leather armchair, turned around three times, and then settled in, looking across the room at them expectantly.

"She prefers the chair," Hope said decidedly, with a serious face. "But don't worry, she hasn't shown any signs of being a chewer."

"Okay. She can have the chair. But let's make her a bed. Before she chooses where she wants to sleep, too."

Hope gulped as she followed him into the bedroom. More windows, bringing in the sky, the trees, the sunlight. The bed was enormous. Hope looked away, not liking how her pulse picked up at the sight of it. She needed a psychiatrist, that was all.

The "old blanket" turned out to be an almost brand new designer quilt from the guest bedroom. Noah Brandywine simply didn't have "old" possessions. But he eagerly folded it and put it into the corner of his bedroom, and she gave him points for that.

"Here, Hair. Come check out your bed," he called.

And Hair eagerly did, plopping down onto the Yves St. Laurent quilt like she belonged there, which evidently, she did.

And seeing Hope standing in the center of the large room, wearing a bright red sweatshirt and her blue jeans, a brilliant spot of color in the middle of his elegant but colorless world, his heart began to ache. He knew that she belonged there too.

He had everything, everything he had ever aimed for. He had reached every goal that he had ever set. Except the joy of life, the aliveness that he felt when he was with Hope. She brought color to his life, confusion . . . feelings.

They walked the dog, got her settled, and headed back for the clinic, where Hope knew she had a waiting room full of clients, both furred and feathered, who wanted her care.

As they passed the imposing structure that was Brandywine Beauty Products, one question kept echoing in Hope's mind. *Where was Manny?*

Chapter Nine

W*here am I?* thought Manny, as he tried to open his eyes to the blinding light. It hurt a lot, and he squeezed them shut again. So much light. So much pain. Where was he?

His ears began to function. Voices in the distance. The clatter of metal equipment. An intercom droning. He listened hard. "Dr. Marucci, Emergency Room, stat." "Dr. Johnson, please call 2110." He swallowed hard. He was in the hospital.

He tried to open his eyes again. The light was still too bright. His head ached. He tried to move—bad idea. Pain jolted through his body. He squinted. He could move his head from side to side and see around the room. There was a person sleeping in the bed next to him. He could hear the even breathing and see the shape of a body under the blankets.

The clock on the wall said seven o'clock. Was that morning

or night? It was dusky out the small window, but that could be morning dawning or evening setting in.

He could move his arms a bit, but they hurt like anything. He had strapping around his chest. He guessed he had a broken rib or two.

His leg. His leg was the source of the greatest pain, after his head. He could feel the cast that encased his right leg, covering his foot, and ending in the middle of his thigh. *Thing must weigh a ton.* He sighed heavily. Well, at least that part was over, and he had lived.

As his mind cleared, he could guess the scenario. He was in Brooklyn. Probably at Victory Memorial.

A lot had gone down since he had taken that stupid job at Brandywine, determined to put an end to the animal dilemma, and thereby saving Hope's stubborn neck before she got herself hurt.

His stomach clenched. He hadn't solved a thing. He had only made it worse.

He had started out with the premise that he would prove that Brandywine Beauty had nothing to do with the fiasco, and what he had proved was just the opposite. But he only had half the information. And the rest was out there, like a vial of nitroglycerin, just waiting to explode.

Manny shook his head, disgusted with himself. He had thought going undercover into the plant was such a good idea. It was as dopey as any of Hope's unbrilliant plans. They had known who he was the whole time. It had been only coincidence, not brilliant detective work, that had resulted in his overhearing the phone call, made by the guy he had been hired with. "Duke" had discovered that someone named "Perkins" was onto something about the animal testing.

"MarcoPolo," he had heard the guy whisper into the phone. "It's Perkins, all right. He's working for the feds. I should take him out? I can blame it on the kid. Convenient that he's here, eh? Get moving on it. Get him picked up right away. I'll take care of this one, and then take care of her, too."

It was that phrase that was killing him. Was the "her" Hope?

He had hustled to warn the guy in danger, but he had been seconds too late. He had heard the gun shots. He had seen the body tossed into the river.

And then they had seen him. And they had grabbed him, and he had known he was a goner if he didn't get away. So he had fought with every ounce of his strength, and he had gotten free, losing his wallet and all his money in the scuffle.

But he hadn't waited around to retrieve it, knowing that although he had evaded the bad guys, the good guys were going to be after him soon. He'd gone into a panic, knowing that he'd be picked up in minutes. He knew what would happen to a kid with his history accused of a violent crime. He knew about prisons, and being poor, and having no one to stand up for you. So he ran.

He ran as fast as he could. Out of the factory, out of town, out on the highway, where he'd snagged a ride with the first car that stopped, and hadn't stopped running until he was on the Jersey Turnpike and headed back to New York.

It was somewhere between Exit 9 and Exit 10 that he had grown up, and grown up for good. As they said in the cartoon, "Are you a man or a mouse?"

He'd run from trouble all his life. He'd run from a bad home to the bad streets. He'd gotten involved in the gang thing, and when he couldn't stand it anymore, he'd run from that, too, instead of standing up and facing it.

He would have never stopped running, if it hadn't been for Hope Highfield and her darned animals. She'd never asked a thing from him, just offered love and acceptance and a mission in life, holding it out to him like a carrot until he bit and saw he could have a second chance.

But he knew he had mucked that up too, because now he'd be accused of a crime that he had no defense against. But worse than that, he'd left Hope in danger, especially if she didn't stop meddling, which he knew she wouldn't.

So he had made a vow that the first thing he would do after getting out of the bread truck that had offered him a ride over the Verrazano Bridge and into Brooklyn, was to call Hope quickly and tell her what he knew so far, so she'd be wary.

And then he was going to do what he should have done before he ever left Brooklyn. He'd wanted to leave the gang— but he knew the way out was a painful one. He hadn't wanted to be "jumped out," hadn't wanted to pay the price, so he'd run. But sometimes a man has to stop running and face the consequences. As of now, he was in danger in New York, and for a different set of reasons, he was in danger in Pennsylvania. A man could run out of places to live, at this rate!

So he would call Hope, and make her safe; then he would face the gang, and fight his way out. And then, he would return to Pennsylvania, to fight his way out of that mess too. And while he might lose these fights, he would know he had done what he thought was best. Which was what Hope had told him, to be true to himself.

He jumped a bus when he ended up in Brooklyn, putting almost all of his remaining change into the slot for fare. He held onto his last quarter, to call the operator to make a collect call to Hope.

The bus had groaned to a stop at the corner of his old neighborhood, the night streets wet and glistening under the grimy streetlight. He stepped off the bus, and headed for the pay phone at the corner by the drug store.

He didn't make it. It was just his luck that the gang had picked that particular moment to rob the pharmicist on the corner, and were just heading out the door with their loot as he stepped onto the curb. They saw him.

He didn't make his phone call. But a while later, he soon learned, a passerby used the same phone he had been heading to to call an ambulance, and they had taken his unconscious body to Victory Memorial.

As his mind cleared and the memories came back, panic set in. How long had passed since his "jumping out" attack by the gang? How long had he lain in the hospital? And how was Hope, since he hadn't even been able to make the warning phone call to her?

He reached an aching arm to the side of the bed and pushed the call button. In a few minutes, a dark-haired nurse appeared. She was wearing white nurse's pants, white shoes, and a col-

orful nurse's tunic bearing pictures of Winnie the Pooh all
over.

"Ah, you have returned to the land of the living. That is
good." She reached over and clicked off his call bell.

"I hear you were jumped out by the Banderos. That true?"

He smirked. "Maybe."

"Well, if that's the case, you are lucky to be here. I hope
you learned your lesson and stay clear of those guys. The last
few they jumped out didn't fare so well. They left in a box.
You got off easy, with that broken leg and a few busted ribs,
and, of course, a good hit in the head. You must have a head
like a brick."

"I've heard that before."

Immediately, she took his hand, and began to take his pulse.
He jerked his arm away.

"Don't bother with that stuff right now," he said gruffly,
wincing from moving his arm too quickly. "How long have I
been here?"

"Two days," she said. His stomach clenched.

"I gotta get to a phone. Get me a phone."

The nurse clucked her tongue and began to take his pulse
again. He practically growled.

"Listen, buddy," she said, looking at him with wise eyes.
"You do what I want, and then I will do what you want. Hold
still. Pulse first. Phone second."

Hurting all over, he obeyed. She also took his blood pressure and temperature, checked his cast and his wrapped ribs,
and lectured him some more about the consequences of a life
of crime. It made his head hurt more, but he took it.

Then silently, she walked out of the room, returning almost
immediately with a phone that she plugged into the wall.

"Go ahead, make your call. But there's no long distance.
You got to call collect."

He sighed, said a prayer that he wasn't too late, and dialed
the operator.

"And stay in bed, Mr. Busy on the Phone. You have one
heck of a concussion, and you're going nowhere fast. If you
have to stand up, you ring and get help, you hear me? Or you

will be having a meeting with the ground. Don't press your luck."

But pressing his luck was just what he needed to do. He needed to warn Hope. The operator tried to put the call through, but the answering machine picked it up.

"This is Doc Highfield's office, Frances speaking, and I'm just too busy to take your call right now, being that absolutely nobody but me seems to believe that they need to work around here. However, if you are calling for an appointment, Hope will be having an open clinic today from one P.M. to four P.M. and again tomorrow from nine A.M. to noon, so just show up if you need to see her. Don't bother leaving a message. If I'm too busy to answer the phone, you better believe I'm way too busy to listen to the message too. Bye."

"The party isn't answering to accept the collect call, sir," the operator said.

"Yeah, I hear," he said, with resignation.

"Try another number," he said, giving the number of his foster parents. The line was busy. Somebody was gabbing on the phone, as usual.

"Anything else you want to try?"

"No, I guess not. Thanks." The only other option he could think of was calling the police, and when he did that, there'd be hell to pay. He'd give Hope another shot in a short while, just in case. As long as she was still holding office hours, at least he knew she was okay so far. He tried to calm himself with that thought, but it didn't work. He had to go home.

With a start, he realized that Ryerstown, and the life that he had built there, had become home, and there was a tightness in his throat at the thought. Whatever he had to face when he got there, he would face. But first, he had to help Hope.

Boldly, he sat up in bed, trying to ignore the surge of pain to his head with his movement. His cast was large and hard to manage. He gingerly swung it over the side of the bed, the weight of its descent almost making him crash to the floor. He grabbed onto the IV pole beside him. The tubing jiggled wildly. This was going to be tricky. He couldn't bend, due to the tight strapping around his chest. He could barely move the casted leg, due to the weight and unbalance. Whenever he moved, something hurt. He held onto the IV pole, which had wheels on its base. Inch by inch, he pulled himself up to a standing position. His blue pinstriped hospital gown hung awkwardly, partially open in the back, exposing his butt to the world. He grimaced, but ignored it. This was not the time to get shy and self-conscious. He was on a mission to find a pay phone.

With determination, he took a tiny step forward, half dragging his cast. Pain shot up to his hip. His head felt like rockets were being launched against the inside of his skull. He took another tiny step, his jaw set. Nothing was going to stop him.

Nothing but the floor, that is. On his third step, the pain got the better of him. He drew in a deep breath, saw a black sky with twinkling stars fill his vision, and hit the well-polished hospital floor with a clamor. He had passed out cold.

As Hope returned to the clinic, she thought of the woman's scarf on the table and felt the beginnings of a respectable-sized knot in her stomach. She could just imagine the woman who had left the scarf. She had seen pictures of Noah in the society pages, with the elegant beauties on his arm. Ever the handsome dashing bachelor.

She sighed out loud as she maneuvered the Suburban into the driveway of Hope's Haven. He was not *her* handsome dashing bachelor.

She looked down at her freshly scrubbed but unelegant hands on the steering wheel. She hadn't had a manicure in years. She had never worn Brandywine perfume. And she certainly didn't care *who* had become scarf-free at the house of the dashing Noah Brandywine. Did she?

But she couldn't deny the feeling of . . . what? Envy? Curiosity? Resentment? And she was too honest with herself to forget that fluttery feeling he caused when he was near, when he touched her, even when she was mad at him.

Which she was at the moment. But it didn't discount the fact that she was, for some strange reason, feeling pretty bad about herself.

She pulled the car to a halt at the clinic door, realizing how much she had been hoping to see Manny's bicycle leaning in its usual place beside the wall. But of course it wasn't there. And if he had shown up, by any chance, he would have been picked up immediately and thrown in jail. People were jumping to conclusions about Manny, too.

She listened to her answering machine. Appointments needed, medicine to be refilled, questions about new kittens. There were several hangups on the tape, as if someone had tried to call and had hung up when the machine answered. She would probably hear from the annoyed clients tomorrow. The last message was from Meridith. She dialed her friend back.

"I need you tomorrow. Don't say no."

Hope sighed. When Meridith began a conversation with "Don't say no," it was going to be a doozie.

"Ok, I'm sitting down. What is it this time? You want me to give a manicure to your friend's bird again? Explain reproductive rights to the couple who were fighting over custody of the bulldog again? Or it it something better this time?"

Meridith laughed, and the sound of it made Hope smile. Meridith had a great laugh.

"Much better. I'm just reminding you. You said you'd go. Tomorrow night is the night I am getting a big award from the City of Phildelphia. And dinner and dancing at the Four Seasons Hotel downtown, compliments of the mayor."

Warning bells went off in Hope's head.

"Hmmmm. I'm not sure they want an ex con there . . ."

"Don't say hmmm. Ex con or not, I need you to come. I do not want to go by myself. It will not kill you to get dressed up for once and do this one little thing for me."

One little thing? Hope made a face and stuck her tongue out at the phone.

"Gee, Meridith, I might have plans. I might be incarcerated again by then."

"No matter what you do, I swear I will bail you out. But you have to come with me."

Hope did not want to go. Hope hated the political and social events that were a part of Meridith's busy life. But Hope loved her friend, and she knew she would not have asked if she didn't need her by her side. And it was lovely that Meridith was getting the award. She would go.

"Shopping, hair, and nails tomorrow. Appointments are set."

Hope swallowed, looking down at her hands again. Nails?

"Well, okay," she heard a voice that must have belonged to someone else say. "I'll do my vet appointments in the morning and pick you up at noon." She swallowed again.

There was dead silence at the other end of the line.

After a minute, she said, "Mer, are you still there?"

"Who are you, and what have you done with my friend Hope?" Meridith was laughing again. "This will be wonderful, but you must be gloriously ill. You would never in your right mind agree to hair and nails, let alone shopping, Hope. Are you alright?"

"Fit as a fiddle. But probably not in my right mind. So you are taking advantage."

"My right as an attorney. We always take advantage. So how did I win this one? Was my argument that persuasive?"

"Nope," said Hope, almost under her breath. "I agreed because of the scarf."

Meridith's lively laugh erupted again. "Well, I know better than to ask too many questions. I'm just glad you're going with me. You can explain tomorrow."

When she hung up, Hope sat staring at the phone, feeling quite awful inside. She'd explain it whenever she figured it out herself. Which wasn't going to be any time soon.

Exhausted, she made the rounds of the animals at the clinic and made sure that everyone was settled. Then she turned the answering machine on again and left the office quickly. She entered her apartment, stripped off her clothes, and climbed into bed, exhausted.

"Go to sleep, go to sleep," crooned the parrot from the living room. "Shut up," Hope crooned back. And went soundly to sleep.

Chapter Ten

"You're out of your blooming mind!" Hope's eyes were wide and horrified, staring into the mirror from where she sat in the hairdresser's swivel chair. Her eyes locked in the glass with Meridith's, who stood boldly behind her.

"I will not cut my hair short. I will not layer it, perm it, frost it, or put it in a blender. Case closed, counselor."

Meridith sighed and tossed her head, giving up. She knew when to push Hope and when it was hopeless. The look on her face indicated hopelessness to a high degree.

"Well, okay Ramon, just give her a wash, trim, and blow dry. But get rid of those split ends. And conditioner—lots of conditioner."

Meridith had this way of making her feel like a dog on the way to a dog show . . . a dog who was going to lose. . . . But she bit her tongue. She'd take the trim—and the conditioner—and she'd get out of here.

Two hours later, she got to take off the horrible lavender smock that she had worn for the ordeal, and emerged from the door with a shiny head of freshly trimmed hair. Still the same color, and more or less the same style. She caught a glance at herself in the glass reflection of the department store they were nearing. Well, maybe a bit more style. Compared to . . . well, no style. She smiled. She looked down at her hands.

They were her own nails. She had drawn the line at donning nail tips, much to Meridith's consternation. She wouldn't want to have to stand up to Meridith daily in a courtroom in a life or death matter. Nail tips had about done her in.

But her hands looked wonderful, she had to admit. The nails were shaped, and buffed, and painted the lightest shade of soft pink. They looked—feminine. She smiled, pleased in spite of herself.

"In here." Meridith steered as they approached the main door of the sprawling department store.

"Well, this is going to cost me," grumbled Hope as she allowed herself to be led to the elevator. They stepped out on a hushed floor. Their feet sank into the lush, dark red carpet. To the right of the elevator, two elegant mannequins were strategically placed—wearing black linx fur coats.

Hope turned to Meridith in fury, eyes flashing.

"Whoops!" said Meridith. "Didn't mean to come in the "dead animals on hangers" door. Sorry. Can't we sneak by?"

"Can't do it, Meridith. Can't shop here and promote the death of innocent animals. Get me out of here."

Meredith rolled her eyes, but nodded her head. Hope was Hope. There were other places to shop.

They settled on a quaint little dress shop on Chestnut Street, where vintage dress designs hung side by side with current designers. Meredith chose a long black formal, with elegant lines, beaded spaghetti straps, and a short satin jacket that would give sense of formality when she received her award.

Hope chose a navy blue knit dress, with a square neckline and simple lines. It hung to the floor in soft, flowing folds, accentuating her curves with every move she made. She topped it with a fringed shawl in a colorful print.

At the end of the afternoon, toting dress and shoe bags, they stopped for a quick dinner at a cafe near Meridith's downtown apartment. Hope watched her lifelong friend across the table. Her award tonight was symbolic. As much as Hope's mind was filled with thoughts and worries about Manny and the problems in her life, she was glad she had spent this uncharacteristic day with Meridith.

"Will we be the only women there without dates?" Hope asked, slurping the last drink of soda through her straw.

Meredith made a face.

"Hope, do you still have to slurp? Where are your manners? Well, we'll probably be the only ones without dates under the age of sixty-five."

Defiantly, Meredith slurped her soda, too.

"Probably because we slurp. Remember how your mother always complained that we would never have a man because we acted as if we were brought up in a barn?"

Meredith laughed out loud. "We're just strongminded, Hope. We made the decision to live life our own way a long time ago. It takes a very strong man to accept a strong woman."

Hope slurped again. "Especially one who slurps."

"Let's get out of here," said Meridith, throwing a large bill down on the table. "And Hope." She turned and looked at her friend. "It means a lot that you are coming tonight, especially with all you have going on."

"Glad to be there to celebrate you, my friend. And I promise I will be on my best behavior."

"Even if the mayor's wife shows up in a genuine leopard-skin pant suit?"

"Don't push your luck. Remember you're dealing with an ex con!"

* * *

When Manuel Perez woke up again cognizant enough to care what day it was, he found out it was Saturday. The mid-morning light was streaming in through the blinds at the small hospital room window and a nurse's aid was carefully re-hanging a fresh IV bag on the pole near his left shoulder.

"It's Saturday, eleven A.M.," she answered his question. "You gonna keep your butt in bed this time? They all gettin' tired of patching you up in this place."

She smiled, and her face lit up with a white, toothy grin.

Manny tried to smile back, but it hurt. Nevertheless, he was not going to keep his butt in bed. He was going to get home to keep Hope safe.

Without a moment's hesitation, he reached over and plucked the IV needle from his arm, wincing as it came free.

Gingerly, he swung his good right leg over the side of the bed, his bare foot touching the floor. With two weakened arms, he helped to slide the heavy cast from the bed. It hit the floor with a slight jar. He took a deep breath, feeling his lungs push at his taped, pained ribs. He was far from well, but a long way better than before. This time, he didn't try to walk immediately. He grabbed the portable IV pole, using it as a staff. He pulled himself slowly to his feet, giving the blood in his body time to circulate. The room spun, but he did not black out. Progress.

When he was as steady on his feet as he was going to be, he took a tentative step toward the closet for his clothes. He walked ten feet. It felt like ten miles. He opened the closet door and pulled out his jeans and chambray shirt. So far so good. He was going to get out of here.

He turned and started the long trek back to the bed. He pulled the swiss army knife out of his jeans pocket, and in one fluid motion, sliced the side of his jeans leg open.

The cast slipped through, but the pants leg hung loosely around the cast. He cut a strip of the bedsheet and tied it around his casted leg, holding the pants leg in place.

"A fashion statement," quipped Manny as he buttoned his shirt. In the closet, he found a pair of crutches. They were a little short. Busily, he lengthened them.

He moved to the elevator, every step an effort.

"Oh, you're leaving?" said the nurse's aid at the busy desk. "I guess I missed that on the chart. You take care now. And make sure you stop at the business office on the way out." Manny left the hospital on stolen crutches, determined to hitch a ride, and he did not stop at the business office.

A person would have to be half dead not to appreciate the music at the Four Seasons Hotel, Hope thought.

The dinner had been delicious, much better than the usual chicken and rubber peas served at many large political events. And Meridith had sparkled as she was awarded her plaque with the Mayor's loquacious praises. Even Hope's eyes had been teary to see Meridith so happy. It had been worth the trip.

And then dinner was over, tables graciously cleared, and Philadelphia's elite had hit the dance floor with gusto.

Hope looked over to Meridith, as they watched the other couples at their table rise to join the dancing ranks. Meridith looked wistful.

"Well, some things never change, eh?" Hope said with a grin. "We're at the dance, but still we sit. Reminds me of Miss Panarelli's dance class, all over again."

"I was thinking the very same thing," said a deep, resonant voice from right behind them. She saw Meridith's face light up.

Hope turned and was startled to see Henry the nerd-turned-Congressman, looking sensational in a black tux.

"Henry!" she exclaimed.

"Well, hi!" said Meridith. "I didn't see you here."

"Just arrived," said the Congressman. "We had an emergency session that ran over in Washington, but we sped right home the minute we could. Sorry I missed the presentation. I hope they took pictures."

"It was a press event. They took a million," said Hope. "I'm glad for once it's Meridith who will be in the paper. She didn't even have to get arrested to get press!"

"But, of course, I also didn't get to kiss Noah Brandywine," laughed Meridith.

Hope could feel her cheeks color, thinking of that picture of her, in Noah's embrace. For once, she was speechless. She looked daggers at her friend.

"How about a dance?" Henry said happily, ignoring the look, and putting his hand out to Meridith.

Was that Meridith blushing?

"Well, no. I couldn't leave Hope here alone at the table. And I don't suppose that threesome thing we used to do in dance class would be appropriate at this event."

At that instant, Hope wished she was invisible.

"Hey, you two go dance. I'm going to go locate the ladies' room. Then, of course," she laughed and said truthfully, "I shall go crawl under a rock as the only woman in the room under the age of eighty who does not have a partner."

"But you do have a partner," came another low voice from the man who had come up behind Henry. "And if you won't dance with me, I'll be forced to crawl under the rock with you. And think of what the press would do with that!"

"Noah?" Hope's voice was like a squeak.

Noah Brandywine stepped forward, putting a hand out to Hope. "Yep, it's me. And I think it's safe here. Not an animal in sight. Except the political kind."

In his tux and crisp white shirt, he was the handsomest man in the room. Hope felt her mouth go dry. She felt the funny feeling in the pit of her stomach start up, the way it always did when she was in his presence.

This man was bad for her. There was something about him that made her giddy. She said, thought, and did things in his presence that were not planned. She didn't like that. She was *not* going to dance with him. She would not give the press another opportunity to splash her face across the newspaper. She would simply refuse. Being around Noah Brandywine was like having your heart used as a ping pong ball.

She just couldn't, wouldn't, take it anymore. No more letting her heart get bounced around. She knew better than that.

"I'd love to," her voice said, completely ignoring her rational brain, and she floated from the chair and into his arms.

See? See? the voice inside her head protested. Her body would not obey the logic of her mind. Hope Highfield, ping pong ball extraordinaire, sighed softly, and did not object as he pulled her gently onto the dance floor and tucked her close to his chest.

The music swelled. Colors and laughter swirled around them. Flashbulbs popped. *At least,* the little voice inside of her stated, *your hair looks absolutely great this time.* And then she allowed herself to melt in his arms.

Noah was a wonderful dancer. Hope followed his lead, and they blended into the kaleidoscope of couples moving around the floor.

"You look absolutely gorgeous, Hope. What a dress!" His voice was soft, and his breath tickled her ear.

She could feel herself blushing. "Thanks. You look pretty sensational yourself. I'm surprised to see you here. And Henry, too."

She looked over his shoulder to see Henry and Meridith glide by.

"Henry has certainly improved since eighth-grade dance class!" She giggled.

"So he admitted on the way over here. Told me about how he used to dance with you both."

She couldn't help laughing. But then a realization hit her. "On the way over? You came together?"

She pulled her head back and looked at him.

"Whoops." He grimaced. "I think I just blew the plan."

"The plan? You knew we'd be here?" Her realization hit another level. "Even Meridith?"

Meridith convincing her to get her hair done, her nails, her dress. Meridith pleading for Hope to support her. Meridith! Anger started to swell.

"Down, tiger. Don't wreck the mood. The intention was pure and good."

He pulled her close and placed a soft kiss on the hollow of

her neck. The angry feeling ebbed, replaced by a different feeling, one she couldn't define. But it left her knees weak.

"Meredith thought if you knew, you wouldn't show. She really wanted you to be here. And she wanted Henry . . . and I wanted—you."

His arms tightened around her, and his mouth nuzzled her neck again. She breathed in the wonderful Brandywine cologne, and felt the soft hotness of his breath on her neck.

Later, maybe, she would be mad at Meredith. Later, maybe, she would be angry about the plan hatched behind her back. Later.

Right now, she just wanted to dance forever.

Manny was too tired for words. Since crawling out of a bread truck that had taken him across the Verrazano Bridge, he had stood on the side of the road a short distance from the turnpike entrance, leaning heavily on his wooden crutches, one thumb extended, trying to hitch a ride.

No one seemed to be exactly jumping at the chance to pick him up. And time was ticking by.

He wasn't exactly sure how long he stood there, but it was long enough for the optimism he had felt with Luis's assistance to wear off, long enough to feel aching in every bone of his tired body. It was long enough for the afternoon hours to turn to dusk. Headlights were soon lit on the cars whizzing by.

Despair, fatigue, and disillusionment were doing a dance in his head. But when he was actually considering lowering himself to the ground to rest before he literally collapsed, he was startled back to attention by the blast of a truck's air horn. He stumbled to the side of the road. Was the driver trying to run him over? It wouldn't be the first vehicle that had attempted that on this disastrous day, but it would definitely be the largest.

The truck that was pulling up beside him was a full-sized semi, its giant black cab gleaming in the light of car headlights that passed by. On the side of the door, a pink lightning bolt was brashly painted. Underneath the slash of bright paint, the name, "Curtis Wenk, Bernardsville, PA" was neatly painted. Chrome bumpers gleamed in the light of passing cars as the truck bore down on him, standing exposed on the side of the highway.

Manny noted the details as the monster truck slowed to a stop exactly alongside him, brakes squealing with the friction.

The truck came to rest only inches from his casted leg.

"You doin' physical therapy there on the shoulder of the road, or you lookin' for a ride?" The country voice drawled at him from high above, a face appearing in the cab window. In the background, he could hear music blaring—"Proud Mary," with Tina Turner's voice exploding from the radio.

"A ride would be good," said Manny evenly, assessing the man's face.

There were kooks everywhere in this world, including the cabs of semis. And Manny did not need another fiasco on this day that had been so horrible so far. But in the light of the cab, the trucker's eyes looked friendly and understanding. The man seemed okay.

"Where you heading?"

"I'm going down the turnpike and across the bridge into Pennsylvania. I'm from the Pocono mountain area, and I'm bringing a load home. Where you aiming for?"

"Pennsylvania. A town called Ryerstown."

"I know it. I'm not going that far south, but I can get you pretty dang close. Hop in. You can keep me awake. I've been driving all day and I'm too tired to tango."

Manny thought quickly and decided he didn't have many options. He would take the ride from Curtis the Proud Mary-playing truck driver and go as far as he could. Every mile driven, he would be that much closer to Hope.

He limped around the truck to the passenger side and climbed up onto the running board with a loud grunt. His ribs ached, his head swam.

"Hold on, Buddy," said Curtis, reaching over and opening the door for him. "You look like you got hit by a semi. You okay?"

Manny landed in the seat with a sigh, his body thankful to rest.

"I'm okay, but I've had better days. Thanks, man." He extended his hand. Curtis shook it.

"No problem. I've been in bad spots myself. And I could use the company, like I said. Course, in my case, I had a fight with a bull. Used to ride rodeo."

Manny laughed. "No bull for me . . . well, maybe Full of Bull. Some bad guys who had it in for me. Nothing that won't heal."

Curtis slammed the rig into gear and pushed the gas pedal to the floor. The truck roared with power, wheels turning, engine revving, and they started to move. The music blared. Proud Mary ended, and another Tina Turner tune began to wail.

Manny watched out the high window as the truck zipped along, the mile markers flashing in the headlights, the distance ticking by, bringing him closer to Hope.

Curtis may have had retro music tastes, but he was definitely high tech. A CB radio squawked constantly on the dashboard, alerting him to state police speed traps, traffic snarls, and occasional trucker jokes. An electronic radar detector was mounted beneath the rear view mirror. A greenish computer screen flashed a road map, where he could keep track of his route and possible detours.

"Neat stuff," said Manny as Curtis demonstrated his gadgets.

"Thanks." The trucker smiled. "You know, you look kind of familiar. You ain't someone famous, are ya?"

"Afraid not." Manny said, blushing in the dark. *Infamous maybe, but not famous.*

"I got a TV that works in the cigarette lighter," Curtis boasted, proud of his varied equipment. "When I have to stop to grab some shut-eye, I can see the news."

Oh man, thought Manny. *No wonder I look familiar. My face is probably plastered all over the news.*

Suddenly, a blast of Beethoven's music filled the cab. Curtis scrambled in the compartment between the seats and pulled out a cell phone.

"Hello?" he yelled into it, over the Tina Turner CD and the roar of the engine. "Howdy dear. Yes dear. Ok dear. Bye dear."

With a thumb, he flipped the phone off. "The little woman. Wants me to bring her cat food for the cat on the way home."

Manny stared at the cell phone in his hand. "Curtis, can I make a call?"

Curtis chucked him the phone. "Go ahead. That's what it's for."

With trembling finger, Manny dialed Hope's number. It rang a few times, and the answering tape came on with her familiar message.

"Hope, it's me, Manny," he said with urgency. "I'm on my way home, Hope. I've been laid up, but I'm okay. Tell my foster folks. And be careful, crazy lady. Brandywine Beauty Products is in this up to their necks. I didn't kill that guy. But someone sure did—and it was to protect what's going on over there. Watch your back, Hope."

He pressed the button and disconnected the call, a feeling of hopelessness coming over him. Was he too late? Could he protect Hope? And from who? He wasn't even sure. He looked up and met Curtis's thoughtful eyes.

Here comes trouble, he thought quietly.

Curtis leaned over and flipped off the CD player.

The silence was deafening.

"I just figured out why you look so familiar," Curtis said, squinting a little as he turned toward him. "You been like the cover boy of the paper lately. Seems like you're the guy everybody's been looking for. They're accusing you of some pretty bad stuff."

Their eyes met, in the silence of the cab.

"I didn't do it, man," Manny said quietly into the void.

"Well, I reckon I know that, somehow," said the driver, running his hand through his sparse and well-oiled hair. "I reckon I know that if you had done such a thing, you woulda been hitching the other direction. And besides, you got those eyes. Eyes of a fair man. You didn't kill nobody on that river, did you?"

"No. But I'm immersed in it up to my eyeballs. And this woman doctor who has been so great to me is in a lot of danger, with the attention she's brought to this thing. I'm going back to help clear this mess up."

Curtis stared straight ahead.

"And it looks like I'm harboring an accused felon. Obstructing justice. Accomplice after the fact."

Manny sighed. The last thing he wanted to do was to get any more innocent people in trouble.

"Just let me out here, man, and don't blow the whistle. I'll go on my way. Just give me a chance to help Hope."

"Now you hold on a daggone minute, you young stallion. You didn't hear me say you should get out of this rig. You didn't hear me say I was going to turn you in. I was just stating facts. I am harboring an accused felon. I am obstructing justice. I am an accomplice after the fact. I'm also hauling four thousand pounds of tomatoes. Those are just facts. Don't be afraid of the facts, young man. Big deal. The question is: What are we going to do about it? How are you going to help this young lady? We have to think."

He reached over and flipped the CD player on once again. Tina Turner's "Proud Mary" filled the night air.

"One thing's for certain. I think better with Tina in the background. Don't you agree?"

"Whatever you say, Curtis Wenk." Manny sighed with relief, as the truck ate up the miles, barrelling down the highway.

It had been a set-up for sure, but Hope decided she wouldn't even complain about it. They had choreographed the night like a ballet. Henry and Noah had arranged for separate cars, at Meridith's suggestion, and after the band played the last romantic song, Meridith asked Hope if she minded riding with Noah, as Henry had "volunteered" to take Meridith home. She was happy for her friend, who obviously was enjoying her time with the classmate-turned-congressman. She agreed.

It had been a wonderful evening, right until they were ready to head out the door. She was walking, her arm loosely through Noah's, when a tall, elegant blond suddenly blocked their way. Her mouth was smiling, but her eyes were flashing.

"Noah," she stated succinctly.

"Cheryl. How are you?" he replied politely.

The tension in the air was thick and obvious.

"As if you care," she said with a flip voice, adjusting her scarf and pulling her lightweight jacket into place. Her escort, a slight and silver-haired man in a black tux, offered her an arm to lead her out the door ahead of them.

Hope's stomach tightened. The tall woman had poked a hole in her fairy tale night with only a few words. She was tall, and gorgeous, and elegant. She obviously had a history with Noah. Only it wasn't ancient history. Hope knew that she must have seen him very recently. Because she was wearing the very scarf that Hope had picked up from his dining room table only yesterday. Hope recognized the pattern and the quality. And the type of woman that Noah was famous for attracting.

Which was not exactly the same type as Hope Highfield.

She put her fantasies to rest, and decided to be mature and self-controlled. She would take the ride home, and leave Meridith to her good time. She deserved it. And Hope would live through it.

She found herself getting into Noah's Jaguar, and waving to Meridith and Henry as they drove off. She settled back into the soft leather seat, pulling her shawl around her shoulders calmly, still humming the last song, which was echoing in her head.

Noah got in beside her and instantly the car felt very full. His presence seemed to envelop her.

"You sure look wonderful tonight, Hope."

"Thanks." She looked at his strong profile as he drove the car. "You look pretty good yourself."

He looked natural in a tuxedo, sophisticated and comfortable. He turned his head toward her, his eyes twinkling with a boyish grin. "I almost didn't have a tuxedo to wear tonight.

Hair climbed up on the bed while I was in the shower, and decided the tux laying there needed an additional pressing. I thought I'd never get the creases out."

Hope laughed.

"Uh oh. What did you do to her?"

"I told her to get her own darn tuxedo."

He reached over in the midst of their laughter and took her hand. Her breath caught in her throat.

"You have me mesmerized, Dr. Highfield. And, by the way, thank you for turning my house into a rain forest. The plants look good. Of course, I will probaby kill them. I've never had much luck with nurturing living things."

She was oddly touched by his admission.

"You're welcome. The dog, the plants—I think you will do just fine." Her eyes twinkled. "Besides, I didn't know what to do with them. They were a thank you gift for Georgia and her puppies. And you had a part in the success of that delivery. Only fair that you should have to water the plants."

Noah stroked her palm, sending shivers up her arm.

She didn't want to think about scarves or elegant nasty women, or mysteries, or missing people. She just wanted to feel.

The minutes passed quickly, and the Jaguar purred gently into Hope's Haven. Her senses were swirling as Noah turned off the car engine and turned to her, his arm coming around her and pulling her close.

"Hope, I don't care if the whole staff of *USA Today* is hiding in the bushes with a flash. I just want to kiss you. All night I have been driving myself crazy thinking of this. I need to kiss you so much."

She didn't object. Not at all.

His mouth came down on hers then, tenderly touching. She let out her breath slowly, feeling his lips upon hers. Without hesitation, her arms came up to his shoulders, then around his neck. The kiss was mutual and powerful. She was floating in the sense of him. His arms tightened around her, and she reveled in the closeness, the feel of his heart beating beneath his starched tux shirt.

He was the first to pull back. When his face was no longer touching hers, she felt an absolute sense of loss. He lessened his grip.

"You make me crazy, Hope. I've never felt like this."

He looked sad for a minute.

"But I'm not sure that you believe in me. Totally and absolutely. That I would never do anything that would hurt you. Some day you will be sure. Some day you'll believe in me."

She couldn't argue. She wanted his words to be true. She didn't want to face all the questions that she had. She wanted to stay secluded with him in the darkness of the car, feeling these feelings, reveling in the touching, enjoying the closeness with him.

But he was right. She sighed.

"Well, it was a fabulous night." She opened the car door to get out, and he quickly came to join her, walking her to the door.

She hadn't left a light on, so the first thing she saw when she entered the room was the red blinking light of the answering machine. Automatically she hit the button, and the first message began to play.

"Hope, it's me, Manny." Hope held her breath and listened. When she got to his indictment of Brandywine Beauty Products, she felt her heart quicken. She saw Noah's face harden, his mouth becoming a taut line.

She stood staring at the machine as it finished.

"I do not have anything to do with this, Hope. You have to believe me."

She felt tired. Total fatigue. She was hugely relieved that Manny was coming home—and not welcoming the legal stink that would ensue. But at least he was okay. And when he got home, he would explain what he knew. She looked at Noah. She stared into his eyes.

And no matter how hard she tried, she could not believe that he was involved in the animal testing. She could not believe that he was a chronic liar. With a certainty that glowed like a hot ember inside of her, she knew that he was telling her the truth. Whatever Manny was talking about, the Noah Brandywine that she knew was simply not involved.

How would this mess ever be straightened out? What could be the answers? With Manny coming home, they would sooner or later find out the truth. But it was going to get ugly. And she just didn't want ugly right now. She wanted to reclaim the peace and happiness she had felt in the car. She would face the coming craziness later.

"We'll find the answers sooner or later, Noah. I do believe you."

Happiness flooded his face, and he pulled her into his arms.

"We will find out what's going on, Hope, I promise."

"Let's take a walk," she said. With the swirl of emotions she felt, she didn't want him to leave. She didn't want to be alone with her thoughts and her fears.

So they walked. They walked down the driveway, toward the riverbank, under the twinkle of a million stars. The air was cool and fresh. The moon reflected on the flowing river. They didn't talk. After they had walked a while, they stopped along the grassy bank.

"Want to sit? I do some of my best thinking on this riverbank." Hope plopped down on the grass in her long dress and slipped off her shoes.

Noah hesitated a slight moment and then sat beside her.

She looked over at him with a grin.

Noah Brandywine, CEO of Brandywine Beauty products, elegantly sporting an expensive tuxedo, was sitting in the grass on her riverbank.

"You hang around with me, buster, and you are going to continue to ruin a lot of clothes."

He chuckled and took her hand. "Good thing I'm rich."

"Good thing."

There was a flash of white behind him, and he had the strangest sensation of hot air blowing around him. Startled, he turned his head.

"ARRRGHH!"

Billie the Goat stood right behind him, breathing her not exactly fresh breath down his neck. Now she was face to face with him, her big eyes gleaming, her hair standing up in all directions around her face. Her mouth was open, and her tongue was lolling.

"Hope, the goat!" Noah cried in dismay.

"Yep, that's the goat. She must have gotten out of her garage. Go away Billie. That's a girl."

The goat turned and sauntered away, stopping to chomp on a tuft of grass as she went.

"My heart will return to my chest now, maybe." Noah had broken out in a sweat. "I'm not sure I will ever get used to that goat."

"Sure you will," Hope said with a laugh. "She has a way of growing on you. Kind of like a barnacle."

"Well, you are definitely more optimistic than I am."

They sat in silence then, watching the river flow by, and held hands, taking strength from each other, knowing that the storm would come.

Chapter Eleven

Manny stared at the glowing dashboard of the truck as the minutes passed. They had traveled many miles south on the turnpike, exits flying by, as Manny had told Curtis about his plight and the events that led up to it.

Curtis was a good listener. He didn't say much. But once in a while, Manny could see his forearms tighten on the steering wheel, making his giant dolphin tattoo swell as the muscles tensed.

"Bottom line is," Manny said in a tired voice, "that Hope was right. Brandywine Beauty is behind the animal testing. Something is going on there. And I wasn't the only one snooping. This guy who was shot, he was nosing around too. So I guess they thought they'd get rid of two problems at once. He is dead, and I'm on the run.

"But I still don't know that Noah Brandywine is the one

responsible. Something deep down in my gut says that he isn't. But somebody is, and one way or another, I have to keep Hope safe until it's all sorted out."

Curtis looked thoughtful.

"We better call the cops. Let them know that she's in danger."

Manny swallowed, knowing he was right. No matter what the risk to himself, he had to protect Hope.

A minute later, Curtis had him connected with the Ryerstown Police Station.

"I'm calling about Dr. Hope Highfield, the vet who's involved in this Brandywine Beauty Products problem. She's in danger." Manny's voice was strained.

The police officer sighed, and then said, "Look, buddy, this department has been busy with Hope Highfield and her shenanigans for days. She's not in danger. She *is* danger. You hear me?" The cop sounded tired. "She's got a problem, she can call me herself. Or better yet, call when I'm off duty."

Manny was furious. "Look mister, somebody's already been killed in this mess, that guy they found in the river. Hope better not end up that way too, or there'll be hell to pay."

"Hey," said the officer, suddenly serious. "Who is this anyway?"

"This is Manny Perez. And you guys better get out and do your jobs."

"Oh sure, buster, we'll do our jobs, all right. The first of which is to lock you up. Where are you?"

Manny pressed the off key, disconnecting the call.

Manny tossed it on the seat. "Well, that wasn't exactly successful. We got to do something for Hope."

"Well, you left the message for her, but a message ain't enough," the trucker said thoughtfully. "That little lady might not get the message. But even more likely, I don't think she'll worry about it. She isn't going to accept that she's personally in any real danger. But the truth is, as I sit here thinking about it, with you out of the picture, seems to me that the culprits would see her as the only loose end to tie up. I don't suppose the cops will do anything. The cops—well, they are just small town cops. We got to get their undivided attention."

Manny sighed, so loud it could be heard over the whine of the eighteen-wheeler. "So what do I do?"

"Well, in the mountains, we do a lot of fishing. . . ."

Oh boy, thought Manny. *What's coming now?*

"And what fish you get depends a lot on the type of bait you use. You set up the line in a special way, in a special place, and you draw the fish you want right away from anybody else who is cluttering up the stream. It's a matter of the bait, boy."

Manny turned and looked at him in the dark, his meaning coming clear.

"I think you're saying that I'm a better bait than Hope. I know more. I'm more dangerous to them. Put me on the hook, and they'll leave Hope alone."

"You know, for a dumb gang kid, you're pretty dang sharp." Curtis tossed him the phone. "Climb on the hook, Manny boy. Time's a wastin'!"

Manny got the number for Brandywine Beauty from the operator. He dialed it determinedly, and followed the taped instructions for leaving a message after hours. "Noah, this is Manny. I have no idea if you're behind this, but I know what's been going on there, and I'm not going down for this. I'm back in town, and I'm ready to take you on or anybody else I need to. You want to deal? I'm on my way and I'll be in touch."

He took a deep breath.

"And nothing better happen to Hope, or I'll be singing like a bird."

He hung up abruptly. He was glad the darkness hid the fact that his hands were shaking.

"Well done, my man." Curtis raised his arm and slapped Manny a high five. "One way or another, you've made it worth their while to leave her alone. Since you're still around, she's not the only threat. And if you're onto them, they wouldn't be able to get away with it. They don't know how much you know."

Manny rubbed his hand over his face. "I wish I knew if Noah was involved. I just don't want to believe that."

"Time will tell. And you've bought her time. But you've put yourself out of the frying pan and into the fire. Now not only will the cops be on your trail, but the killers as well. You gotta protect your butt."

"Well, I don't exactly know how I'm going to do that. I feel like my butt is right out there and exposed. But if it saves Hope, the heck with my butt."

The truck barrelled down the highway, and a big green sign came into sight. They were taking the exit that led to Pennsylvania. Just ahead, Curtis would be heading west toward the mountains, and Manny would be heading south toward Ryerstown.

Manny shifted in his seat. "Well, man, looks like this is where you and I part company. There's your exit. Let me out at the toll booth and I'll try to flag down somebody going farther south. And thanks." He extended his hand.

Curtis just looked at his extended hand and then ignored it. Instead he picked up the cell phone again. Buttons beeped.

"Dolores? How ya doing, baby? Me? I'm fine. But I got a little job to do, so I'll be home late. Call Dan and tell him that his tomatoes are fine, but delayed. I got to help a kid help a vet who saves little animals. What? You like that? I thought you would. You want I should bring you a kitten? Okay, baby, we'll see. Gotta go now."

The phone made a beep as he was about to hang up. A red light warned "Low Battery." Curtis dropped the phone with disgust. "These things go dead right when you need 'em every time."

The truck barrelled past Curtis's exit.

Manny smiled with relief. "You taking me further, Curtis?"

"All the way, Manny boy. That was the Missus. She agrees. The tomatoes can wait. And if not, Dan'll have enough spaghetti gravy to last a lifetime."

"Thanks, man." He felt a glimmer of hope.

"No problem. I wasn't always a trucker carrying vegetables, you know. Did a stint as a union roofer, years ago. Also did a stint in Vietnam, which was no picnic, let me tell you. I know what it's like to be up against trouble, up close and personal. You got to have somebody to watch your back and that's the truth. Tell me where the heck this Ryerstown is and we'll get there quick as this rolling salad can make it."

"Two more exits on the interstate," Manny said with emotion. He hadn't known how alone he had felt until he had been given help.

"Okay good buddy. But now, we gotta get some more assistance. Even old Curtis can't pull off this maneuver alone. You're going to have people all over you like maggots in summer. I got to contact some people."

"But the phone is going dead."

"Forget the phone, man. Don't need the phone for this. This is a job for real men."

With a laugh, he grabbed the CB radio, punched a button, and said gruffly, "This is Curtis the Dolphin man. SOS. I need help man. Who's out there?"

The radio crackled back. "Gotcha, Dolphin man. This is Bernie Bear. What's your marker?"

"Hey Curtis, Snake here. Wazzup man?"

"Ralphie calling Curtis. Ready for action."

Curtis smiled at the amazed Manny. "You gang kids aren't the only ones who stand up for their friends, you know." He laughed again and turned back to the radio. "Anybody ready and able, head toward a town called Ryerstown. We got a little problem that might take some muscle. Turn to channel sixteen for details."

He stretched and cracked his knuckles, and the dolphin tattoos flexed again.

"Now this is what I call backup. You're about to get a little escort into town, Manny boy, just to make sure there's no funny business til this all gets straightened out."

At Brandywine Beauty Products, the man sitting at Noah Brandywine's large imported desk picked up the phone as the programmed machine had begun taking Manny's message. He listened without making a sound, fury building in his chest.

"I don't believe it!" he growled as he heard the message, a strong fist banging down on the shiny desk surface. "Stupid punk," he said out loud in a gruff voice as he sat in Noah's leather desk chair, a snifter of expensive brandy in front of him. "That little creep could wreck everything." He dialed a number.

"Trace that call, and tell me where it came from. Spare no cost, and don't waste a second. I want to find that little troublemaker and stop him in his tracks. And don't mess up on this. I can't believe you didn't take him out when you had the chance. Don't mess up again."

Within two minutes, the phone rang again. "The call came from a cell phone. Phone is assigned to a trucker named Curtis Wenk. Came outta central Jersey somewhere. Phone's not on and traceable anymore."

"Must have picked the kid up on the highway. He must be heading this way. Maybe he's in a truck. Find the sucker. You hear me? And then find the vet and get rid of her, too. No more mistakes. Too much is at stake here!"

He hung up the phone and looked across the room to the blond who sat with her long legs crossed in a seductive way. "Looks like the party's over, Cheryl. You might think that little vet who took your man away is a pain. We'll take care of her. But her little assistant is ten times worse. He's going to bring the whole operation to a halt if we don't stop him. This just raised the stakes."

Frank Johnson, the security chief from Brandywine Beauty, stood up. "Go home, dollface, I'll call you later. I got to do some damage control at the plant."

Cheryl pouted and stood up, her scarf around her neck as she pulled her coat over her shoulders. "This was not a banner night."

"You can say that again, dollface."

He followed her to the door, watching the seductive way her expensive hips swayed as she moved. His body reacted. She had been Noah's woman, and now she was his. But for how long?

Anger rose inside of him at the thought of all that was at

risk. Noah Brandywine had everything. He, Frank Johnson, just wanted a piece of the pie. It had been a clever scheme, stealing Noah's concepts and formulas for new product research and trying to beat Noah Brandywine to the punch.

Noah, with his slow and steady, much too careful development plan. Frank had found the glitches in less than half the time, by using those pathetic animals, and was well on his way to making products that he could launch in his own, brand new company.

He had stolen Noah's woman, his formulas, and now he'd steal his business. He grimaced. The job here at Brandywine was done. Except for that little know-it-all punk, and that big mouth vet. Time had run out.

He picked up the phone and made a last call.

"We're done. Get the truck right now and move the test products before anybody knows what they are looking for."

The voice on the other end of the phone grunted in agreement.

"And then torch the place. Make sure there's no evidence left for anybody to put this thing together. I want to see Brandywine Beauty Products become a pile of ash on the ground."

Something about a gently flowing river in the moonlight can calm the soul. Hope and Noah sat on the grassy bank, feeling the late night breeze and watching the reflection of the moon on the water.

For Hope, it had been an evening she would always remember. The spinning dance floor, the feel of Noah's tux against her cheek, the smell of his aftershave when her face nestled against his neck, it had all seemed so natural and so right. There had been ups and downs, the appearance of the scarved blonde with the icy voice, the telephone call from Manny.

Life was just not simple. Some minutes she felt like she was whirling around in a hurricane of problems. Other minutes, like these stolen ones on the riverbank, she felt peace.

The other emotions seemed like the alien ones. The worry about Brandywine Beauty and Noah's involvement, the fear for Manny and his legal problems—as she sat on the river-bank, the truth of her beliefs began to flow over her. She knew in her heart that Manny was innocent. And the truth was, she knew in her heart that Noah was, too. Somewhere, somehow, there were answers to the problems at hand, and they would be found.

Noah held her hand, gently stroking it as he looked out over the river. She looked at his profile in the moonlight, and felt her heart swell with an unfamiliar gust of feeling. She loved this man. She swallowed hard.

Love was not a new emotion. She loved many of the people in her life, some of them intensely. She loved her life, her practice, her furry clients, even her gruff and judgmental father. She was no stranger to love.

But this, this was different. The feeling she had for this man who was gently holding her hand was a new one. This was a different kind of love.

Softly, she laid her hand over his, and he stayed still for a moment. Then he turned and looked at her, and she saw the emotion that was clear in his eyes. Slowly, gently, he brought his face to hers, lips touching, breath escaping. She closed her eyes, basking in the beauty of his touch.

He covered her lips with gentle kisses, then her cheeks, her eyelids, her forehead. His hands travelled up her arms, pulling her into his embrace, as his lips found hers again.

There was less softness now, as an urgency grew, and the pressure of his lips began to increase. Held close to him, she could feel the beat of his heart, almost feel the blood coursing through his veins. His lips claimed hers, and then moved in-sistantly to her neck, making her shiver. . . .

This time, there was no photographer to explode distracting flashbulbs in their faces. There was no crowd to witness their action. It was just the two of them, in the moonlight, in the beauty of the night. A groan escaped Noah as he kissed her again. She kissed him back with a passion that exploded inside of her, surprising her and filling her with wonder. She loved this man. Her hands came up to his face, fingertips softly exploring, feeling the slight roughness of his beard, the crispness of his shirt collar where it touched the back of his neck. Noah. This was Noah.

His arms held her close to him, his hands traveling up and down her back, encircling the smallness of her waist, awakening her body like an electric jolt at every touch. She pressed close to him, her breath becoming shallow.

She loved his touch. She longed to melt into him, totally. But a small voice in the back of her brain pulled her back, back through the kaleidoscope of feelings and sensation.

"Noah, please," she said, the words taking every ounce of strength she could gather. She pulled back, distanced herself a small bit. She felt the loss of his warmth, the contact with his strong body. Yet she knew that she was doing what was right. "We have to think."

His sigh was frustrated. "I know. I know." His hand moved to her hair, smoothing it with his fingertips, plucking one loose curl and putting it behind her ear. "We have time for this later. I just feel so strongly . . ."

She blushed and smiled, meeting him word for word. "Me too."

"And I'm not going to make any mistakes here, Hope Highfield. This is a long term proposition. This is life."

Hope laughed. "You make it sound like a business deal— or a life sentence."

"Well, it is for life, Hope. I don't want any less."

He stood and pulled her to her feet, wrapping his arms around her again. "We'd better go. Or I'm not sure what will happen on this riverbank." He kissed her lightly. "We have a lot to talk about. About you. And me."

Hope had the sudden vision of the icy blond at this evening's event. And of the distinctive scarf she wore around her neck. The scarf that she had seen on Noah's table. Reality hit her like a wave. Her emotions tumbled. Her feelings were so strong for this man. But she could not allow herself to be simply another woman on his arm, casual and forgettable. Was she? She could not stand the thought of that.

"You, me, and the blond," she said softly, watching his face in the moonlight.

"The blond?" He looked puzzled. "Ah, Cheryl. Hope, there is no one else. That is over. Way over."

Way over? "Noah, I saw the scarf she was wearing tonight on your dining room table yeaterday. How way over could it be?"

Noah stared at her, question in his eye. He thought for a minute. "Well, I don't doubt that she could have left a scarf at my house in the past. But believe me, she did not get it yesterday or today. If you recognized that scarf, she must have another one. She hasn't been at my house."

He ran his hand through his hair. "I am asking you to accept so much, Hope. To trust me about other women, no matter what a field day the press may or will have. And most of all, to trust me about Brandywine Beauty Products. I am telling the truth. I have never authorized experimentation on an animal in my life. And I never will. You have to believe in me."

"I do." As she said the words, she felt him stiffen in her arms.

"I don't believe it," he said woodenly.

"I do believe in you." Her back was to the river, she could see his face in the moonlight. He looked shocked.

"No, Hope. Not us. I believe in us. But I don't believe that."

He turned her around, so that she was facing the river, looking directly across at Brandywine Beauty Products on the opposite riverbank.

Lights were moving in the parking lot of the factory, and in the moonlight, even at that distance, they could see a large truck that had pulled up to the building and was backing up to a side loading dock.

"There are no deliveries or shipments scheduled for tonight."

Noah's voice was firm and steady.

They stood motionless, looking across the water. In an instant, lights could be seen going on though the lower windows.

"Someone is in the basement. Something is going on in that plant. My plant." His voice was angry.

Hope didn't say a word. She stared across the river at the truck, his words seeping into her.

"I don't know what is going on there, Hope, but I'm going to find out. If this animal trouble has originated at Brandywine—well, I don't know what I am going to do."

He pulled her to him and hugged her tightly. "I'm sorry, Hope. I'm going over there to bring this thing down, one way or another."

"I'm coming with you."

"No way. There's no time to lose arguing. I'll call you when I find out what's going on."

Hope had visions of the man who had been pulled out of the river. Her memory flashed to Manny's troubled voice on the phone. This was serious.

"Can we call the police?"

"Not yet. I need to go and see what's happening. Even though I'm not behind this, it's going to be disastrous for Brandywine Beauty Products. I've got to go see what I'm up against before the whole thing blows up."

"Well, you don't have much time. It will take you over a half hour to drive there, down into town and across the bridge. And if they know that you are onto them, God knows what they will do to any animals left in their care. They must know that Manny is heading back. The truck is already there. They'll be watching for you."

He looked at her thoughtfully.

She went on. "Let's take the boat, Noah. Straight across the river. Like George Washington crossing the Delaware and surprising the British. Quicker, and quieter."

He turned to where she was pointing—at the rickety green rowboat that sat at her dock.

He paled. "Uh, Hope. I don't know how to row."

She took his arm and pushed him toward the boat. "Well, thankfully, I do. And now is as good a time as any to learn."

He followed her to the boat, swearing under his breath.

In the darkness of the truck, the radio crackled again.

"Curtis, you pain in the butt. This is Danny. What are you up to with my tomatoes? You get yourself and that rig back here right now. I want my tomatoes delivered. This is my first subcontracting job with Highfield Trucking and if this load ain't on time, I'm gonna lose this contract, and it's coming directly out of your sorry hide."

"Don't get your shorts in a knot, Daniel," said Curtis with a chuckle. "You listen to me quick. I was hoping you were working on a Highfield contract. I got a major problem here. You get on the phone to Highfield Trucking and get a message to the old man Highfield himself. Tell him his daughter is in danger, and he better get himself on the phone and get the stuck-up Ryerstown cops to get their blue behinds out to her place to protect her. And I'll protect your darn tomatoes. Over and out."

The rowboat had been painted dark green long, long ago, which could be deduced only by the flaky patches of paint that still remained. It had two benches, and two sets of oars resting in place.

"Come on," said Hope, hiking up her dress and stepping into the boat with one foot, pushing off the bank with the other.

"Are you nuts? We are going across the river in that thing? It can't possibly float, Hope. For God's sake, look at it!" Noah pointed at the questionable craft with an incredulous tone in his voice. "In case you have failed to notice, that is not exactly a yacht!"

Hope pushed an escaped lock of hair firmly behind her ear, lifted her chin defiantly, and glared at him.

"Don't start with me, Brandywine! There is something going on over at that plant, and you need to find out what it is. This is the only way. Someone has been killing and maiming defenseless animals, and *I* intend to find out who. Plus, someone got shot, Manny's life is in tatters, and so is yours if we don't find out who is doing this."

She stepped the rest of the way into the boat, just as it began to move with the current, and grabbed a set of oars.

He stared at her. "You're serious."

"Serious as a bear in a beehive. Get in the boat."

He sighed. He knew she meant what she said. He was going

in the green flaky tub whether he liked it or not. Because he was not going to have her go alone, no matter how dumb the plan. He stepped toward the boat.

He lifted one foot into it. The boat slid the rest of the way down the bank. He attempted to lift his other foot into the boat. The boat had other ideas. It jerked with the current, and he almost lost his balance, having a sudden vision of himself sitting in the water. He grabbed the edge of the boat. He would not go down. With a wobbly twist, he tried to steady himself. His valiant attempt was a success—more or less.

He caught himself, foot dangling momentarily in the air, then plopping down beside the boat, firmly planted into the muddy sludge at the edge of the river. Water filled his imported Italian leather shoe. With all the poise he could muster, he pulled his foot free from the muck. It slurped as it came up.

Grinding his teeth, he climbed the rest of the way into the boat and sat on the rickety wooden bench at the rear.

The boat was moving away from the bank, partly from the current and partly due to the fact that Hope was vigorously rowing. He looked at the gray wooden oars and flexed his hands.

"Hey, Makeup Man. Think you could give me a hand?" Hope said over her shoulder. "You know, row, row, row the boat?"

He smirked, and picked up the oars. In for a penny, in for a pound.

"Ouch. I got a splinter. These oars are awful."

"Well, it's not the Queen Mary, I'll admit."

She watched him struggle to find a rhythm with the oars.

"This is not as easy as it looks in the movies," he said through clenched teeth.

From his rear position, he could see Hope's shoulders move in rhythm, her arms strong and easy, her oars cutting through the water. He tried to match her. How exactly did she do that?

By the time they were halfway across the river, his arms were aching. They were not only rowing across the river, but also against the current, which tried to carry the craft downstream.

"It's important to keep up the impetus, Noah," she called between breaths. "Right down river there are some awful rapids, and this rowboat would be reduced to planks in no time."

"Argh!" he called back. "I don't think it's much more than that now. Remind me that I never want to take a cruise, okay?"

"You got it," said Hope, not breaking her rhythm.

He grunted.

"You never rowed before?" she asked between strokes.

"I guess it's obvious. And what were you, a Navy Seal?" he said with embarrassment.

She laughed, in spite of the tension of their mission.

"Women's Crew team, University of Pennsylvania. The boats were a bit different, but the coordination is the same! You're doing fine. We're almost there."

Which was true. Within minutes, they had pulled up to the darkened dock behind Brandywine Beauty Products. Hope stepped foward and anchored the boat by its aged rope.

Gingerly, Noah stepped out of the boat, his one wet foot squishing with each step as they made their way to the plant.

Noah punched in a code on the keypad near the back door at the lower level of the building. The steel door opened. Hope followed him inside. Most of the building was dark, but looking down the long corridor, they could see light shining from an open door. They headed toward it.

"This is a storage area down here. All these doors should be shut and locked." Noah sounded angry. "I can't believe this."

They reached the lighted doorway, and when they stepped inside, Hope caught her breath.

The room was lined with metal shelves from floor to ceiling. Florescent light shined overhead. They contained row after row of shiny metal cages—animal cages—and they were not empty.

Hope could hear her heart doing the jackhammer thing in her chest, anger pumping through her veins with every pulse. She turned to look at Noah.

His face told her what her gut already knew. He was horrified, and surprised. His mouth was set in a firm, tense line, his jaw clenching. In that glaring florescent light, she realized that she knew two things for sure.

One was that he had not been a part of whatever was going on, here in his very own factory. She knew this with the certainty of knowledge that makes people trust in their beliefs through death and disaster. She trusted this man.

The second thing was more personal, and equally as mind boggling. She absolutely and totally loved this man.

She instinctively held out a hand to him. He stared at her extended hand for an instant, almost in disbelief. He knew what it meant. He knew what these animals meant to her. And he knew that she did not blame him.

His dark eyes filled with tears. Later, he would face the issue of blaming himself for not knowing what was going on in his own company. Later, he would find a way to fix the damage done. But now, with the fervor of a man reaching for a lifeline, he took that hand, his large hand grasping her tiny one tightly, and felt a sense of profound gratitude.

They walked into the room. Once inside, the silence that they had experienced in the hallway was broken. Little animal sounds filtered through the air from the residents in the small cages. Kittens meowed softly, hamsters scampered and made little scurrying sounds as they approached. A line of baby rabbits stared solemnly at them, making no noise at all.

As they stepped near the rabbits, she saw the telltale rows of fur shaved, the lines of colored dots where they had been test injected or exposed in a chemical test. In another row of cages, small kittens were almost bald, their skin red and inflamed from reaction to a test chemical.

I think I'm going to puke, Hope's body decided. *Not now,* her brain responded. *No time for puking.*

She took a deep breath and willed the rage to subside.

"We've got to get them out of here."

Her voice was clear and calm. She went into doctor mode and began checking the animals.

Noah's brain was buzzing with thought. Manny's message

... the truck that had pulled up by the loading dock ... Hope's determined investigations ... the body floating in the river ... this illegal and unethical project was rapidly coming to a dangerous end. The brains behind it would be panicking and ready to shut down, destroy all evidence incriminating them, including the innocent animal victims, and most probably arrange for Noah to be blamed in the process. *There is very little time.*

He crossed the room to the single desk and picked up a clipboard, scrutinizing the pages it contained, deciphering the tests, the chemical formulas, the products tested. There were several products that he recognized from his own Research and Development team, products in the early stages of consideration, products that someone was planning to steal and market by speeding up the testing and beating Brandywine to the punch.

The formulas had been carefully locked up in Noah's house, protected by his intricate security system. He thought of that system; he thought of the scarf that Hope had declared had been in his house only yesterday.

It had been a clever plan—and obscuring it from Noah's watchful eye had been a feat that not too many could have pulled off. Noah clenched his jaw as the puzzle pieces came together.

I know who is responsible.

Should he call the police? He didn't know what was planned. He had no proof other than the very scene he saw before him. Would he, if he were a cop, believe in him, as Hope had done, when confronted by such a sight?

He knew the answer. He thought of the body that had been fished out of the river. He thought of the sick and dead animals. It was easy to dispose of things that were in the way.

He looked at Hope as she bent over a small rabbit, cooing and stroking it as she checked its health. On the one hand, he wanted to grab her and run, to take her to safety. But he knew she wouldn't go. She wouldn't leave these animals.

"It's Frank, Hope, my chief of security. Some security. But it has to be, he's the only one who could have pulled this off.

He's the only one I've trusted with some of this information." He plopped the clipboard down on the desk, the bang echoing in the brightly lit room. "It's just about money. Greed and money. And Cheryl is in on it too."

How many life decisions had he made with money the motivating factor in his rise to success? How many people had he been impressed with, because they had achieved and accumulated fame and fortune? He looked at this woman who was willing to risk it all for a rabbit. Why did her way suddenly seem to make such sense?

"We don't have much time, Hope. The truck is here. They know Manny is on the way back. This thing is closing down and they are going to want to cover their tracks."

"We have surprise on our side, Noah, they don't know we are here. Let's get these animals out of here."

Noah thought furiously. "Can we let them loose? Can they fend for themselves?"

"Not a chance. All of them are babies, and some of them are very weak and sick. I need to get them to the clinic."

"But we need a truck. But if we get a truck, they will hear it arrive." He didn't want to think of what would happen if Frank found them there.

"They didn't hear us arrive, and they won't hear us leave. We'll go in the boat."

Noah swallowed hard. The trip over had been bad enough. The trip back, carrying dozens of panicking animals, sounded like a nightmare. But what choice did they have?

"We need to be sure we have enough time." His mind was clicking into action. He pulled out his cell phone. "I'll call him, give him a job to do. He will think I still don't know what's going on."

"Does he know you went to the dinner? You could tell him you're still in Phildelphia."

He pulled out his cell phone and dialed his own office. He imagined it ringing upstairs. How many times had he made a call like this in the course of business? His mouth felt dry.

Hope turned and watched him, still stroking another little rabbit.

"Frank," he said succinctly. "I was hoping I'd catch you in. I'm still in Philadelphia, went to that award fundraiser event, and I'm still . . . uh, tied up."

Hope couldn't hear the response on the other end of the phone.

"Yeah, she was there. In fact, I'm still with her. She just went to the ladies' room."

Another unheard retort, but the meaning was clear.

"No, I don't think I'm going to get lucky, wise guy. And yes, I'll see what she's up to. I'm not going to let anybody put a slur on Brandywine." Hope saw a nerve jump in the side of his jaw and knew how much self-control this was costing him.

"But I won't be back until tomorrow, which is why I wanted to reach you."

He thought hard, picturing his desk as he had left it.

"I left those trucking contracts on the desk and they have to be handled so they are signed early tomorrow morning. Can you fax them to the subcontractors while you are there? The numbers are included in the contract heading. Get them out ASAP. I want them signed and faxed copies back by first thing in the morning. No exceptions."

There was another pause while Frank looked for the contracts and reported back.

"Tonight, Frank. I don't want a delay. And I don't want to wait til morning."

His eyes hardened as he listened.

"Yeah, just in case I get lucky and come in late. Bye."

He clicked off the phone and turned and looked at Hope.

"Sorry. Guy talk. I couldn't think of anything else to say."

Hope gave a quick laugh, the first glimmer of recovering spirit he had seen since they had entered the florescent lit room. "Get lucky. In your dreams, Brandywine. Come on, let's save some animals."

Chapter Twelve

They had to keep the animals in cages, as there were too many of them, and several were very ill. They consolidated the load, putting as many as they could humanely fit in each cage.

"Sorry, little bugger," Hope said to each as she situated them in their new cramped quarters. "It's for your own good, trust me," she cooed. Noah helped her as much as he could. Sixty animals were still alive. Hope's eyes teared as she removed the ones that had lost their battle with life already, but she steeled herself to return to the packing task at hand. They would save what they could. They ended up with twelve cages, each cage about a cubic foot.

Silently, they made several trips to the rowboat in the dark, each carrying a cage. They spread them out over the floor of the boat, stacking them two high.

The truck was still parked motionless next to the loading dock, with no one in sight. The parking lot lights beamed high overhead, as they always did at night, making the truck visible, and throwing enough light that they could see their way.

Far above, they could see the lights from Noah and Frank's corner offices, and the low glimmer of safety and security lights that remained on in the hallways all through the night.

But down by the back river dock, it was dark and shadowy, and their secret loading continued. The last crates were in place, and they were silently congratulating themselves on a swift and successful getaway when tragedy struck.

The back door of the plant opened, throwing light out into the darkness, and illuminating the boat.

Noah cursed his no smoking policy. A man stepped out, head down as he lit a cigarette on the back entry steps.

It took a minute for him to look up. Hope and Noah stood staring at him, knowing that he would, and that they were going to be discovered. It was inescapable.

Like slow motion, it happened. He stuck the pack back in his blue jean jacket pocket, took a long deep puff, and then raised his head and looked out over the river. Right at the boat.

"Hey," he yelled, mouth still around the cigarette. "Whatcha doing there?"

They didn't stay around to discuss it. Simultaneously, they both jumped into the overloaded boat, picked up an oar, and started paddling.

"Hey," the man yelled louder, first at them and then back into the factory hallway. "Trouble here! On the double!"

They could hear the sound of pounding footsteps as they splashed away from the dock, and more angry bodies appeared at the door.

"Jeez, it's Brandywine, and the troublemaking vet!" he recognized the angry voice of his security chief. "Shoot the bastards."

"Whoa, bad plan," said Hope between hard strokes. "Now would be a good time to call the cops, Noah, don't you think?"

A shot rang out over their heads. Hope didn't even flinch.

Noah was cursing himself for exposing her to danger. If only he had listened to her from the start. "Hope I'm so sorry about this."

Another shot rang out.

"No time for I told you so's!" Hope said through clenched teeth as she paddled with all her strength. "You can make it up to me by the time we're ninety-six, Brandywine! Right now, get on that fancy phone and call for some help!"

She was, of course, right. He pulled out the phone, flicked it open, and got it almost to his ear when the next shot rang out. It hit the phone mid-air, which leapt out of his hand with the force of the bullet, spun though the air as if doing a dance, and exploded into pieces right before it hit the water.

"Geez," he yelled, pulling back his hand. "Did you see what he did to my phone?"

"Paddle, Brandywine, the next shot could be your head. That's not what I call getting lucky."

So he paddled. And paddled. It seemed like they were getting nowhere fast. The boat was overloaded, they were paddling against the current, trying to aim for the soft lights of Hope's Haven without being carried downstream.

Behind them, the shooting had ceased, but they heard the sound of cars revving up, and looked back to see lights leaving the parking lot of the plant.

"They know where we are going," he said quietly. "They are going to drive down into town and over the bridge. We only have about twenty minutes."

He looked back at Hope in the stern of the boat, her rowing rhythmic and strong. His own body was aching from the unfamiliar rowing. They were almost in the center of the river, when the moon went behind a cloud, like a black silky blanket over them, leaving them in darkness.

He swallowed nervously, fear clawing at him. He looked out at the dark, lonely water. He kept paddling, ignoring his aching shoulders. He changed his position, sliding his feet around the crowded cages, and feeling his tux trouser legs stick to his shins. They were wet.

"Uh, Hope, my legs are wet."

"Uh huh."

"And the reason for this is?" He held his breath.

"Twofold. This boat is old and creaky. And we've got it overloaded for sure. But also, the shot before the one that pulverized your cell phone put a two-inch gaping hole in the stern of the boat. Just missed my leg by inches. I stuffed my scarf into it to slow it down, but we're taking on water pretty good."

"So can we fix it? Shouldn't we be bailing or something?"

"I couldn't think of anything effective enough to bail with. I thought we could get close enough to shore, and then bail out. We'll have to let the animals loose, give them a fighting chance . . .

His heart was beating rapidly, just as the moon crept out from behind the cloud again. She saw his face. She had seen that look before.

"Oh no! Noah Brandywine, I see fear there. Are you that afraid of these baby animals? They sure can't hurt you. They can barely stay alive!"

With some amazement he realized he had not been afraid of the animals. It hadn't even crossed his mind. "It's not the animals," he muttered as the water crept up another half inch, making his heart pound harder. "It's the water. I don't know how to swim."

Hope stared in amazement, and then started to laugh. "I keep learning these interesting things about you. I just can't wait to learn more."

She was taking his shortcomings in stride, with humor, even in the face of disaster. He absolutely loved her for that.

"One of these days, maybe something you learn about me will actually be a good thing, Hope Highfield. But meanwhile, can we bail so I don't drown?"

"What are we going to bail with?"

He bent down for a moment, and then handed her something in the dark. "How about an Italian leather, imported, men's size thirteen dress shoe? I have a matched set."

Hope laughed again. "Works for me. Bail, buster. Noah's ark is going to have to make it to shore." They bailed.

The truck made a mighty roar as Curtis downshifted the semi to make the turn onto the exit ramp. A Faith Hill tune crooned on the radio.

"Won't be long now, boy. You can take your heart out of your mouth. Country roads from here on out." Curtis smoothly merged the rig onto the roadway.

A dark cab on a dark night is a good place for soul searching, and Manny and Curtis had exchanged life stories while thundering down the turnpike. Manny grinned and moved his casted leg to a more comfortable position, trying to ignore the itch that kept nagging him from an unreachable spot.

"I really appreciate this, Curtis. Going out of your way like this. And your friends, too."

"It's the measure of a man, Manny boy, when you don't have to run away from problems anymore. When you can lend a hand to somebody just for the principle of the thing. Even for a two-bit punk such as yourself." The trucker guffawed.

"Only kidding. Truth is, you are a pretty cool kid, for what you've been through. Glad to help."

"I'm done running, Curtis. I just want Hope to be okay. After all she did for me, I feel awful that I left her in such a mess."

"Well, we'll see what's going on, and what we can do. He downshifted again and pulled into a truck stop. Three semis sat in a row, and all flashed their lights when they saw them.

"There's the boys. Nice not to be alone when we get to old Ryerstown, whaddaya think?"

He flashed back at them and pulled back out on the highway, this time leading a caravan of trucks. In minutes, they would be in Ryerstown. Manny just hoped that they weren't too late. He started praying hard to a God he had forgotten a long time ago.

"Noah, we're sinking." Hope's words sounded breathless, and she didn't stop her regimen of bailing, then rowing, bailing, then rowing. "We have to let the animals that might be able to save themselves free from the cages." Quickly she started opening the latches.

Noah swore. He had bailed with every ounce of his strength and it still hadn't been enough.

She sensed his anguish. "We gave it our best shot, Noah. Now if you had bigger feet, and therefore bigger shoes, we might have been successful. Or if you wore boots. Did you ever think of wearing boots?"

He stopped, turned and looked at her, and laughed. Only Hope could make him laugh in the middle of a crisis like this.

"Keep bailing, buster," she growled, making a face. He obeyed and bailed.

The healthier of the animals were poking their heads out of cages. Hope was gathering the sickly ones into one cage the best she could.

He had a funny feeling in his chest as he watched her bravely working. He loved this spunky crazy lady who seemed to continually wreck every stitch of his clothes, who interfered horribly in his orderly, successful life, who got him attached to a dog named Hair, who made him face his fears and talk about his past, and who constantly had him surrounded by all of God's scary creatures.

Two small kittens had evacuated their watery cage on the floor of the boat, and had climbed up onto the rickety wooden bench beside him, looking at him curiously with big, round eyes. The funny thing was, he saw as he bailed and rowed with all his might, that he didn't even mind anymore. His heart didn't thump, and the only sweat he was breaking out in had to do with rowing and bailing, and not with kittens. That was a miracle in itself.

The only fear he had was that something would happen to Hope, and that he wouldn't be able to stop it. Like bailing and failing, he would try his best and it wouldn't be enough. The thought gnawed at his stomach, but he pushed it away.

"We're getting closer, I can see the dock."

Hope was back at rowing now, the boat moving even more slowly as they took on more water. "We'll get as close as we can."

And then what? thought Noah, thinking of the dark current and his utter lack of swimming skills.

The moon flitted in and out from behind the night clouds, and their eyes searched for the riverbank when the light allowed.

Something made him turn around and look back at his company on the far shore. As his eyes made contact in the moonlight, he saw the entire plant go black.

"The lights went off at Brandywine," he said softly. "I wonder what they are up to."

Within seconds, it was apparent. A reddish glow appeared in the windows of the basement. Brandwine Beauty Products was on fire.

"They cut the power to stop the fire sprinkler system," he said. "He wanted to be sure there was no evidence."

He swallowed hard.

"I'm sorry, Noah. I know how much that company means to you. But you can build again."

The glow moved upwards now, onto other floors, like a gem shining in the night.

And as he watched it, he knew that what she said was true. It was replaceable. It was just a thing. It was only a person who couldn't be replaced.

He looked across the boat and saw Dr. Hope Highfield, still dressed in an evening gown that was pulled up and anchored around her waist as she rowed, with a sick baby bunny stuck in the cleavage of her dress for safety. If anything happened to this woman because of what had happened at his plant, he would never forgive himself. The heck with the plant.

He took one more look back at his company, the business that had been his heart and soul for as long as he could remember.

Let it burn, he thought. There were more important things at stake. He kept rowing. And praying.

"Uh oh." Hope's voice sounded small in the night.

He looked across to the dock that was now becoming more and more visible. Several sets of headlights could be seen pulling into Hope's Haven.

"We've got company. The bad kind."

The lights were pulling to a stop, and then went out. Over the sound of the river, Hope imagined they could hear car doors shut as the occupants headed for the dock.

Within a minute, there were three figures on the dock. They were all carrying guns, and one had the telltale square shoulders of Frank Johnson.

"We've got to get the animals as close to shore as possible, Noah, so they have a chance."

"They aren't the only ones who need to be close to shore to have a chance," said Noah in a low, even voice. "I am going to sink like a rock."

The empty cages sat on the bottom of the rowboat now, in over six inches of water. Most of the freed animals sat on top of the second level of cages, eyes wide and staring at the rushing water. The cage with extremely weak rabbits and kittens sat on the bench next to Hope.

"I don't think you have to worry about drowning, Noah. They have guns. I think we are going to get shot."

The men on the shore were having a conversation, obviously angry and in disagreement. Then two of the men turned and stomped off, and Hope had a moment of optimism, that they were going to give up their attack.

But not Frank. He stood on the dock and stared out into the black water, finally seeing them.

There was a splash. He spun quickly and saw an empty bench where Hope had been sitting. His heart wanted to jump right out of his chest.

"*Hope!*" he bellowed, staring back into the river. A dark head appeared on the side of the boat.

"Quick," she called. "Hand me the cage of sick animals. I am going to swim them to shore so that they have a chance. They will be watching the boat and they won't see me."

"Sure," he cried sarcastically, in a panic. "Great plan. You will drown with the weight of the cage, I am a sitting duck target in this boat, and then we will all drift downstream and over the rapids."

But he knew he wasn't going to stop her, and he knew he couldn't help her. He couldn't even swim.

"Row, Noah. We can all just do the best that we can do."

So he grabbed her cage and handed it to her, and she took off in the night, bravely doing the almost impossible and keeping the cage out of the water. The moon went behind the clouds again, and he couldn't see her, and he couldn't hear her. And his heart was filled with pain.

But the darkness meant that he also couldn't be seen clearly, so he did what she said. He rowed.

Watching the dark shore, he saw car lights go on once again, and a car started out the driveway. But it didn't get far. Straining his eyes, he saw more lights in a strange array at the edge of the driveway.

What was going on? Over the roar of the river, he heard the haunting sound of a large airhorn, and the lights began moving back down the driveway. Headlights, spotlights, orange running lights.

The escaping car was no longer escaping. It was being forced back down the driveway by an enormous semi-truck that was tooting its airhorn at full blast. And behind it came another semi, then another. Noah stared dumbfounded at the display of lights, wishing he could see better.

And then he could.

The moon escaped the clouds again, and lit up the scene. The lot at Hope's Haven was full of semi trucks, doors flinging open, and drivers hitting the ground running. There was scurrying, while the truckers sabotaged the cars attempting to escape and subdued the men. In the distance, Manny limped on crutches to the office phone.

The dock was visible in the moonlight, and his frantic rowing had brought him less than 20 feet from shore. One lone figure still stood on the edge.

He saw the man he had known for many years, the man he would have trusted with his life, the man he hadn't known at all. Frank Johnson stood at the edge of the dock, hate and desperation etched on his hard face. He stared straight at

Noah, death blazing from his eyes. He was a man who had nothing to lose.

With Brandywine Beauty Products turning to embers behind him, and the woman he loved facing death in a dark lonely river to save some injured animals, Noah Brandywine knew exactly how he felt. He had nothing to lose either.

Noah stood and faced his nemesis.

"Why, Frank?" he yelled at the square-shouldered man. "Why did you feel you had to do this?"

In the moonlight, and with the short distance between them, he could see the dark angry stare of the security chief's eyes.

"I was sick of you being boss, Brandywine. The best cars, the best women, the best looks. I wanted to take it all away from you. I wanted to ruin you. And I have."

With one hand, he wildly gestured toward the burning building in the distance. Lights could be seen flashing around the plant. The fire company had arrived, though Noah knew in his heart that they were far too late.

"I took your formulas, and I took your woman." He snickered. "Or you could say I took your woman, and she took your formulas. Cheryl is mine now. She does what I say."

Noah shook his head sadly. "Cheryl was never mine, Frank. She meant nothing to me. And she isn't yours either."

He felt waves of sadness for the anger and betrayal of the man, but all the time, his eyes scoured the riverbank, looking for signs of Hope making it to shore. His stomach was in a knot. Fear threatened to paralyze him.

Where was Hope? Had she drowned beneath the murky surface? Would she escape the fate that it looked like he was heading for?

Keep the man talking, his mind screamed. Give Hope every second to escape.

Frank's face had clouded for a minute, then he pulled the gun up again. "Well, who cares about Cheryl? Who cares about the company. Just so Noah Brandywine doesn't matter anymore."

He pointed the gun.

Noah looked down into the water-filled boat, which was

barely floating. Several animals had already taken the leap, swimming frantically to shore. Should he jump and take his chances? But that twenty feet looked like a chasm to Noah.

The moon, as if on cue, dove behind the clouds, and the blackness returned, like a protective blanket. And then right beside him, a dark head popped up out of the water. He looked down and stared into the pale face and big eyes.

"Hope!"

"Shhh. Shut up, you bozo, I swear people can hear you in the next county. Noah's bark, that's what it is," she whispered. "I got the cage to shore, now I'm going to try to pull the boat. Keep him talking if the moon comes out again. And one more thing—as soon as we are out of this, promise me you are going to take swimming lessons."

She was serious. He couldn't believe it. She had come back to save him, risking her life. He was afraid of animals, water, failure, and commitment, for starters. She was so brave. Was she afraid of anything? But he wasn't going to have her die on his account.

"Get to shore, Hope. Now."

His low voice was the commanding one, the one that had made him a multidollar success in the business world.

He looked down into her eyes, and saw the love there. She read his thoughts.

"I'm afraid of losing you, Noah Brandywine. That's the worst fear of all. I'm not going without you."

His heart swelled. He had no intention of dying yet. He had a life to live. He had this woman to love.

Havoc had broken out on the dock. Police cars had arrived at Hope's Haven, sirens screaming. There was yelling, and the sound of bullhorns, lights and a crowd gradually making their way down to the dock.

But in the boat, Noah Brandywine knew that they were not going to make it in time. They were not going to be able to stop the one maniacal individual who stood on the dock with a loaded gun and hate in his heart. He had killed before, and he would kill again.

As soon as he could see. And the moon was simply not going to cooperate, to give the police time to reach him.

As the glow of moonlight peeked around the bank of clouds again, Frank Johnson was ready. His eyes strained in the dim light, spotting the boat. Standing at the edge of the dock, he leaned way over, staring into the dark, knowing that he had only seconds to hit his mark.

He leveled the gun at Noah Brandywine, when a small dot of brightness caught his eye. There, in the water next to the boat, the face of Hope Highfield came into view, swimming right next to the boat.

Hope knew the instant she had been spotted. She also knew the instant when Noah had realized that Frank's target had changed.

"Leave her alone, Johnson," he screamed, adrenaline rushing like a blast through his body. "Leave her alone!"

Frank's laugh rang out in the air, as he bent over further to aim the gun at the small figure in the water. Only feet away, it was going to be a clean shot.

As he aimed, and pulled the trigger, Noah Brandywine took action. Without even a thought for his own demise, he leapt through the air, directly in front of Hope, desperate to keep her from being shot.

The sound rang out in the night, and he felt the poker-hot sting as the bullet pierced his shoulder, pain shooting though his body as the dark, deep water closed over his head.

Hope had screamed as she saw him jump. Panic swelled in her, her nerve endings like a million little hot wires as she heard the sound of bullet hit flesh, and heard his grunt as he disappeared under the water.

He had taken a bullet for her. He had dared to face his fear of water just to make her safe. She was not going to let him drown.

The police were almost to the dock, running now, weapons drawn, after hearing the shot. Frank still stood in his spot, his eyes scouring the water. His anger was etched on his face. He was going to lose the war, but he wasn't going to lose this battle. He had gotten Noah, and he was going to get the nosy vet.

Instantly, he caught sight of the woman. Again, he bent over to take better aim. But this time, there was a flash of white on the dock behind him. Billie the Goat had ambled over following the noise and commotion at the dock.

With a short snort, she lowered her head, and did what she always did when she saw a good backside. She rammed straight into Frank Johnson as he leaned over the edge of the dock with full force, completely knocking him into the water.

The shot went wild. With a giant splash, Frank Johnson hit the water. Within seconds, police and deputies were swarming over the dock, pulling him out of the river and getting him into handcuffs, while reading him his rights.

But in the water, the trouble was not over. Time after time, Hope dove down into the water, trying to find Noah. Time after time she arose to the surface, lungs almost bursting, pushing away the anguished cries that wanted to escape from her heart. With a gulp of fresh air, she plunged under the dark river again.

Finally she found him. He had drifted many feet down river, blissfully unconscious, as she pulled him to the surface, yelling loudly as soon as she emerged.

Two truckers had jumped into the water as the rowboat went under, and were plucking wet animals from the current and depositing them on shore. Hearing her cries, the men swam to her, hauled the injured man to shore, and laid him gingerly on the dock.

Hope clamored to his side, pushing the others out of the way. Frantic hands moved over his body.

The wound was a soft tissue injury. She could tell that he had lost some blood, but the shot itself would not be fatal. But the water? Had he been under too long? With shaking hands she felt for a pulse and rejoiced when she found one.

His heart was still beating—but he was not breathing.

Years of medical experience flowed through her, calming her. Carefully, she tilted his head back, checked his airway, pinched his nose, and began to force her breath into his lungs.

Breathe, Noah, breathe. Her mind screamed as she worked.

He did not respond. His chest rose only with the force of her forced air, not his own.

Live, Noah, live! Had he been underwater too long? Was she too late?

His face swam before her eyes, memories of his laughter, his charm, his confusion, his arrogance.

Stay, Noah, stay! Her mind chanted. She loved him. She needed him.

The sound of ambulances warbled in the background. The crowd around them on the dock grew as the moments passed.

Breathe, Noah, breathe! Suddenly, the body beneath hers lurched, and coughed, and Noah Brandywine's lungs began to function, first forcing out the water that had paralyzed them, then sucking in fresh air in strong gasps.

He opened his eyes, and looked up into the eyes of the woman who was perched above him, her face taut with worry and fear.

He remembered hitting the water. He remembered the impact of the shot. He remembered feeling that he was going to die, but that maybe she would live. And that had made it feel okay.

But he had lived. And from the way that he felt, and her presence over him, he knew that she had saved him. The faces around him were a blur, all except for hers.

"Hope," he said softly, wanting to allay her fear. "I'm okay. Thank you." He smiled a crooked smile. "I thought I was a goner. I think you saved me!"

She put her face down to his, with only an inch between them, and answered, "And you saved me. I hope we just keep saving each other, Noah Brandywine."

And then she closed the space between them, and put her lips upon his in a gentle kiss.

At that instant, there was a brilliant flash from above them. They both blinked in surprise, and pulled apart.

"Arggh!" groaned Noah, as he jarred his injured shoulder. Next to them, bulbs still flashing, was the same photographer that had surprised them before.

"Great shot, you two. Great shot," said the man delightedly, still flashing away.

"You better get him out of here before I get up off this dock," growled Noah in a low voice.

The photographer spun and took off down the driveway.

"I swear every time that man takes my picture, my hair is a mess," laughed Hope, as the paramedics helped her to her feet.

They came up beside Noah with a stretcher.

"Oh no, you don't," said Noah, struggling to his feet. He grimaced as he moved his shoulder, but refused to go in the ambulance.

"Time enough for that. Right now I've got people to see."

He turned to find Manny hobbling onto the dock on his crutches, two wet truck drivers on either side.

Walking alongside them was Hope's father, in a pair of striped pajamas and a raincoat.

"Dad? You aren't even dressed!"

Hope couldn't remember ever seeing her father in pajamas, even in the privacy of their own expansive home growing up.

"When I got the message my daughter was in danger I figured there wasn't any time to lose. And there wasn't. This young man and his truckers had the good sense to contact me so I could get the cops here. We will get this business of his all straighened out pronto. Brilliant young man, this Manny Perez. Will have quite a future."

Manny grinned and rolled his eyes.

Hope hugged her father. Then Hugh Highfield turned to Noah and said sternly, "I hope you know what you are getting into with this young woman. Mind you, I adore her, but she's as stubborn as a mule, and as pigheaded as a—well, a pig."

"You better believe it," said Noah seriously.

Then Hugh Highfield's lined face, barely ever used to smiling, broke into a grin. "But life won't be boring, young man. No, never boring. Not every woman can have you barefoot, drowning, shot, burned out, and ruin your best tuxedo in one evening. And have you come back for more. Takes a Highfield to do that!"

Noah smiled and pulled Hope into his arms.

"Yep, I'll always come back for more, Mr. Highfield. She's one in a million."

"That's one in a billion, young man. She's a Highfield, through and through. And now I'm going to go home and get dressed. And don't think just because your business burned that you'll get any better trucking rates in the future from me!"

"Wouldn't think of it, sir," Noah laughed to his retreating back. "Wouldn't even think of it."

"You dove into the water for me, Noah Brandywine! Into the water!" Hope whispered.

"Well, yes, I guess I did," said Noah, running his hand up her arm. "I'm learning that love can make me get over just about any old fear."

"Even Billie the Goat?" laughed Manny.

"Even Billie the Goat. Yep, even that goat is growing on me." said Noah.

"Well, that's good," said Manny. "Because when I came out of the office a little bit ago, she had crawled into your Jag and was gnawing on the leather seat again. She sure likes your car!"

Noah gritted his teeth and looked at Hope, who was trying not to giggle. And then he laughed and kissed her again. No, life would *not* be boring.